Ellis Peters has gained universal acclaim for her crime novels, and in particular for *The Chronicles of Brother Cadfael*, now into their eighteenth volume.

D0950459

Also by Ellis Peters

The Chronicles of Brother Cadfael
A Rare Benedictine
Mourning Raga
Death to the Landlords
City of Gold and Shadows
Funeral of Figaro
Death Mask
Piper on the Mountain
Flight of a Witch
The Will and the Deed

And writing as Edith Pargeter

The Brothers of Gwynedd Quartet
The Eighth Champion of Christendom
Reluctant Odyssey
Warfare Accomplished
She Goes to War
A Bloody Field by Shrewsbury

The Horn of Roland

Ellis Peters

HEADLINE

Copyright © 1974 Ellis Peters

The right of Ellis Peters to be identified as the Author of
the Work has been asserted by her in accordance with the
Copyright, Designs and Patents Act 1988.

First published in 1974
by Macmillan London Ltd

First published in paperback in 1991
by HEADLINE BOOK PUBLISHING PLC

10 9 8 7 6 5 4 3 2 1

All rights reserved. No part of this publication may be
reproduced, stored in a retrieval system, or transmitted,
in any form or by any means without the prior written
permission of the publisher, nor be otherwise circulated
in any form of binding or cover other than that in which
it is published and without a similar condition being
imposed on the subsequent purchaser.

All characters in this publication are fictitious
and any resemblance to real persons, living or dead,
is purely coincidental.

ISBN 0 7472 3600 3

Typeset in 10/10½ pt Times
by Colset Private Limited, Singapore

Printed and bound in Great Britain by
Collins, Glasgow

HEADLINE BOOK PUBLISHING PLC
Headline House
79 Great Titchfield Street
London W1P 7FN

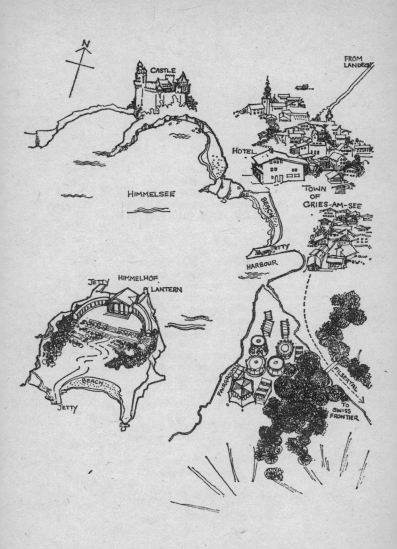

HIMMELHOF AND GRIES-AM-SEE

CHAPTER ONE

The road coiled, breasting the last gentle rise, and idled coquettishly on the crest, broadside to a plane of level grass like a country train at a halt, to allow unsuspecting arrivals to lose and regain their breath on first encountering the view beyond. The upland meadows, here suavely shaped and dazzlingly green, parted and drew back like curtains, to reveal the shallow, symmetrical bowl in which the road terminated, spread out before their eyes in the sparkling air like a sketch-map inlaid with diamonds, all artfully deployed round the single great sapphire of the Himmelsee. Polished and still as a mirror, the lake duplicated the unbelievable blueness of the sky over it. Round its scalloped shores the bright red and bronze-green roofs of Gries-am-See rose tier on tier to the fringe of scattered farms and patchwork fields, then to the foothill fretwork of wooded valleys and terraced alpine pastures, then to the raw, clear colours of outcrop rock, to melt at last into the backcloth of pure steel-and-snow mountains that barred the way to the Swiss frontier.

Una sat up straighter in the back seat of the car, and drew breath in an audible gasp of delight. 'Oh, stop! Please, couldn't we, just for a moment?'

The shoulder of grass, broad as a lay-by and on the convenient side of the road, seemed to have been designed especially for that purpose. An odd circumstance, considering the road itself was a blind way into the hills, originally meant only to serve the network of farms and bring out the mountain timber, long before Gries ever so much as built its onion-domed church. Bearing still more southerly from the south-westerly road between Landeck and Galtür, no doubt it had once dwindled before this point into a rutted cart-track. Now it was a calculated tourist road, well engineered and artfully designed, and the worn grass of this belvedere, honed away into gravel, showed how unerringly it achieved its desired effect.

'But of course!' said their guide, gratified, and the driver wheeled the big car gently to the edge of the slope. No doubt he had had his orders in advance, Una needn't have asked. The young man had the door open for her almost before they were still, and was waiting to point out all the amenities and beauties of his town and its jewelled setting. Lucas followed his daughter out of the car slowly and resignedly, even with a suggestion of reluctance, though she was far too absorbed in the dazzling view before her to notice his reactions. She followed the pointing hand with excited pleasure, fingering the controls of her camera and eyeing the angle of the sun.

'There on the right-hand fringe of the town, you see the castle.' The tall, narrow cluster of Gothic roofs looked just as it had looked all those years ago, the old jetty below probed into the lake like a gnarled grey finger. 'It is partly in ruins, just a great shell, but we keep up the gardens as a public park, and there is a sunken water-garden there, where the brook runs through – so good acoustics, perfect for chamber concerts. Some of the recitals will be given there, in the open air. Even in the evening it is warm enough during July. And beyond, you see the island. From here it looks almost as if connected to the castle pier, but it is nearly a mile out. There was a keep of the Hohenstaufen there centuries ago, but in the eighteenth century they built a small summer palace belonging to the castle. From there just south of the castle our new lake-front promenade runs right round to the harbour.'

The crescent of white, tree-lined road was clear even at this distance, together with its inner crescent of pale, peach-coloured strand, dotted with the bright specks of sun-umbrellas and small beach-shelters. Everywhere along lake-front and square and in the streets of the town there was a curious scintillation that dazzled the eyes, as a breeze from the water, in a noon otherwise absolutely still, fluttered the flags and streamers in which Gries had arrayed herself for her July Festival.

'Our great church, the one there on the square, you must see, it is very fine, and has one of the best organs in Austria, or so we say. There will be a recital on Sunday. And perhaps Mr Corinth would care to try the instrument for himself?'

He had not forgotten his duty to the guest of honour, in spite of his marked preoccupation with Una's delicate fairness, and candid and enthusiastic grey eyes. He turned his undoubted charm momentarily upon Lucas, and recollected that this town he was demonstrating with such proprietorial condescension was the great man's birthplace, even if he had not seen it for nearly thirty years.

'I beg your pardon, I must not let my local pride run away with me. It is for you to introduce Miss Corinth to your native town, not for me.'

'After so long,' said Lucas rather drily, 'you could probably lose me here without effort. Do go on. The place has grown considerably since I left it, and probably changed considerably, too.'

'Your own fault, Lu,' said Una warmly, 'for staying away so long. It's lovely! Why haven't you ever brought me here before?'

It was the question for which his wincing senses had been waiting. He couldn't blame her. It was every bit as beautiful as he remembered it. If the plaster was still falling off the walls in the back streets, as it always had been, and the yards on the edge of the town still smelled strongly of manure, that was not perceptible from here; nor would she care very much, in all probability, when the flaws did come within range.

He need not have worried, the question had been merely rhetorical, and she had already returned her attention to the young man from the Mayor's office. He had introduced himself to them at Innsbruck as Herr Graf's secretary and representative, his own name being obviously of only secondary importance; but Una, after her forthright fashion, had extracted it from him before the car was a mile out of the city. Jörg-Erich Fischer was a very spruce, good-looking, confident young man, with quick, intelligent eyes and a smooth, adaptable manner, quite capable of supplying the whole conversation single-handed if he had to, and quite bright enough to keep his mouth shut and at least seem to be listening if his admirable protective instincts told him it was required of him: the perfect courier and welcoming committee for distinguished visitors. But young enough and human enough to be deflected slightly from his careerist efficiency when a honey like Una happened to crop up in the path of duty. Or sharp enough to understand at once that the quickest way to Lucas Corinth's favour would be through patent admiration of and devotion to his daughter? In which latter case he was soon going to be in some trouble, when it also dawned on him that the way to Una's heart was a reverent detour embracing her adored father.

'Which of all those copper roofs is the concert-hall?' Una wanted to know.

'Just aside from the main square, that big building with the red tiles. Not copper, no. It is quite new, only last year.' It had to be new, there had never been a concert-hall in the old days.

'And is that used for rehearsals, too?'

'The first rehearsal, with orchestra only, will be in the large hall at the Town Hall – that is the long roof opposite the church. But of course Mr Corinth will know it well – this one has not changed at all. Grown,' he said seriously to Lucas, 'yes, the town has grown, as you see, inland in every direction. But the inner town has changed very little. You will find it familiar, I am sure.'

Quite familiar enough, Lucas thought, to set every nerve on edge and start every memory heaving its way out of the past. For a moment his mind recoiled into the craven wish that he had never accepted the sudden invitation to come and conduct his own compositions at the Gries July Festival. He could certainly have mustered another and supposedly prior commitment to make the thing impossible, if he had given his mind to it. But the letter had caught him at a moment of hard communication with his own weaknesses, and he had said yes without giving himself time to turn coward. Twenty-eight years without ever going back! The moment could not be put off for ever. He was here; it was done. Now he had to go through with it, and find out the hard way what kind of Lucas Corinth would emerge at the other side of crisis.

'What's that?' asked Una, pointing. In the blue of the lake, close to the main jetty at the harbour end of the town, a small square of white was tethered, and all its outline quivered with the bright flutter of bunting.

'That's the floating stage we shall use for some madrigal and choral concerts. Herr Graf designed it himself.'

The ubiquitous Herr Graf was not only mayor of the town and director of this first major festival, it seemed, but also the proprietor of the big dairy lower down the valley, owner of a large timber business and a fleet of heavy lorries, and a large share-holder in half a dozen other regional industries. There had always been Grafs in Gries, Lucas recalled, but they had been obscure enough in the old days, small farmers and timber-men like almost everyone else in the district. Evidently one of the tribe had developed an aptitude for business on a bigger scale.

'Our lake, Miss Corinth, is said to be the most beautiful in the whole Tyrol, though it is not very large. It is the setting, of course. The mountains.' He embraced the radiant, icy ring with a dramatic sweep of a long young arm, naming the peaks as he went, – from left to right, to end with the highest and most impressive. 'Vesulspitze – Vesilspitze – and away to the right the Silvretta peaks. Fluchthorn is nearest, and beyond you can just see the Dreiländerspitze and Piz Buin.'

'And beyond all those,' she said, 'it's Switzerland?'

'Yes, that is right.'

She lowered her eyes again from the diamond heights in the sky to the shield of the lake, and the meadows rising from the outskirts of the town towards the foothills. Lucas knew what she was looking for; and she knew enough to look towards the left, to the south and southeast, where the barrier of mountains looked less impassable. 'Which is the path that goes up into the Filsertal?'

She was not asking Jörg-Erich Fischer, Lucas realised; she was asking Lucas Corinth. And there was nothing he could do but answer her fairly.

'Look beyond the harbour, at the extreme edge of the town. You can trace the beginning of the cart-track, a pale line up the meadows, then it disappears in the folds of those first woods. Later it becomes simply a footpath. Look above, where the rock crops out – you see that paler slash crossing it diagonally and vanishing again into the trees? That's the same track.'

'Is it difficult?' she said. 'Could we go?'

'Not difficult until the last stages,' he said shortly. 'In my day it was hard to find beyond the alp, or it would have been less useful, but there was no real climbing until the last half-mile.'

'If you are staying to the end of the festival,' said Jörg-Erich eagerly, 'I hope there will be time for you to see everything. Whatever Miss Corinth wishes, we shall arrange it.' He added, on a tentative note which suggested that he had antennae sensitive enough to have picked up the latent tension in the air: 'There is a small monumental plaque fixed in the rocks now, on the pass. Where you used to cross. The town put it there last year.'

He knew all about that route and its wartime uses, of course, though he surely had not been born when the last fugitives crossed into Switzerland in 1944, at about this time of year. The plaque had been placed, the history had been disinterred and refurbished, very recently, it seemed. After Lucas Corinth began to be a name to be reckoned with in the world of music, as conductor and composer? And after Herr Graf had conceived the ambitious notion of staging a really big musical festival to bring tourism to Gries-am-See? And glory to himself? The weedy young local boy who had guided some thirty-five wanted anti-Nazis to safety in Switzerland before leaving his country with the last of them, one jump ahead of the SS, had been allowed to sleep peacefully for twenty-five years in his chosen exile in England, but when he began to assume the second identity of a composer of world reputation he became well worth polishing and setting up on a small pedestal in his native place. Why not? The bene-fit was mutual. They had made him a very handsome offer to come over and conduct the first performance of his new work here in Gries, and they were going out of their way to provide him with the forces he needed, and of the quality he needed, to make the occasion a success. He didn't grudge being made use of. But he didn't look forward to the accompanying publicity.

'I'd like to go and see it,' said Una firmly.

'I've no doubt Herr Fischer can arrange it for you. I expect to be rather preoccupied with rehearsals, myself. Oughtn't we,' he said rather abruptly, 'to be moving on? I shouldn't like to keep the party waiting.'

'Of course! You're quite right.' The young man

looked guiltily at his watch, and ushered them back to the car. They began the short, descending run into the bowl, in a series of long, well-shaped curves. The fields opened about them as the view foreshortened, harlequin stripes of cultivation hemming the edges of the upland pastures, where the tall hay-poles under their fragrant loads stood like soldiers. The mountains shrank, the lake gradually disappeared, subsiding into its rim of roofs and trees.

'We have prepared only a brief sherry party to welcome you before lunch,' said Jörg-Erich. 'We thought you would be rather tired after the journey, and would prefer to lunch quietly at the hotel and rest until the opening procession begins at three. Then tonight there will be a dinner in your honour at the Town Hall. It is quite a heavy day, so tomorrow you are to be at leisure, and the first rehearsal is arranged for the following day. The orchestra has been studying the work under its own conductor for a fortnight now. I hope everything will be to your liking.'

'I'm sure everything will be excellent,' said Lucas resignedly. He was in it now, there was nowhere to go but straight ahead, and nothing to do but concentrate on the music, which was, at any rate, his one pure and willing contribution. And, perhaps, with whatever energy he had left, on keeping Una happy, and taking her home with none but happy memories of this place which plagued him with such ambivalent recollections.

They were entering the fringes of the town. Decorated shop-fronts rose about them, banners and flowers danced above their heads. There was the usual blaze and flutter of overflowing window-boxes, and the elegant iron and gilt of old craft signs under the gables. Una closed her hand gently about her father's wrist, and said in his ear:

'Lu, where is it? The house where you used to live?'

'Up the hill to the right, behind the other church. You can't see it from the street.'

'You'll show me, won't you?'

It was all exactly as he had foreseen. She would want to see everything, the places where he had played as a child, the cemetery laced with gilded metal-work, where his parents were buried, the school he had attended with so little distinction, the organ in the small church, where he had first improvised. Everything! He would have to shake himself out of his dark abstraction, or she would sense that there was something desperately wrong with this tardy homecoming. He could not be sure that she had not sensed it already. She had all her mother's quickness of perception, as well as her mother's small, fine bones and fair colouring. In a sense she had even performed her mother's part towards him, as well as her own, ever since she was about ten years old.

With all his heart Lucas wished himself away. The very vista of the square opening before him was like the yawning of a trap, recognised too late to be avoided. And yet it had always been inevitable that this visit must take place sooner or later, and the sudden invitation from the festival committee had seemed to him like the finger of fate pointing him sternly to a return he had postponed all too long. It would not improve with keeping. It had not improved with all these years of keeping. He might as well make the plunge, and survive the cold shock as well as he could. Something might even emerge of comfort; his mind might achieve a degree of clarity and stability again.

'We are looking forward so much to hearing "The Horn of Roland",' said Jörg-Erich, recalling his rôle more strenuously as he approached his boss. 'It's a great honour for our town to have the world première. We have gone to great trouble to provide the right soloists – you will meet them at the second rehearsal, or a separate piano-rehearsal could be fitted in first if you prefer – and the augmented orchestra. You will understand that such a work is a severe test for our provincial resources, but I think you will be content – I hope so. Herr Graf has spared no pains.'

'I'm sure I shall be very happy with all his arrangements,' said Lucas mechanically.

'You will find the hall, at any rate, ideal for a concert performance. It would have been a much more difficult task to stage an opera, though we do hope in the future to be able to put on your "Philippina" at Innsbruck, where the lady is buried. But the dramatic cantata form makes production so much easier in this case. I have read the text. Such a happy circumstance for us, that you chose a libretto in German to set.'

Yes, why had he? Purely for the sake of the poem, which had seemed to him to make something bitterly urgent and modern out of the barbaric fate of Charlemagne's rearguard at Roncesvalles? Or had he instinctively fallen back, for his most inward and heartfelt cry against the times and their values, on his first language? He had limited himself in one way, opened a third of the world to his new work in another, and surely exposed himself unarmed to this invitation he was fulfilling now. But the work itself he had loved in the making, and loved no less now it was finished and still unheard. The original *Chanson de Roland*, after all, had been a verse chronicle set to music. For this biting complaint against the waste of gallantry in mutual destruction he had gone back to the original by another way, and found all its elements still there and still valid. You may complain angrily at the squandering of heroism and devotion, but you cannot prefer their inglorious erosion in trivialities, much less their excision from the world as irrelevant.

'I hardly did the choosing,' he said. 'Seifert's poem chose me. I doubt if it will ever be translated, in any case. I doubt if it can be.'

The Mercedes negotiated two sides of the square, and drove through a vast stone archway, solid and plain, into the courtyard of the Town Hall. Jörg-Erich was out of the front passenger seat like a greyhound, and holding the door open for Una while the driver did the same office for Lucas. 'We're on stage, darling!' Una whispered in her father's ear, and giggled briefly to remind him of her childhood, before gathering herself magnificently to meet the reception committee which was advancing upon them down the broad steps from the main doorway. She had time for one brief glance round the court, which was over-hung on three sides by wooden balconies foaming with flower-boxes, and occupied by a concourse of varied humanity more interesting, on the whole, than the descending VIPs.

She saw the fashionable élite of the town, still mar-vellously bucolic, and all the more reassuring for that, deployed in the galleries framing the main face of the building, solid citizen farmers and business men, mer-chants and craftsmen, and their wives, the men in austere black suits as though for church, the women all severely hatted and corseted and gowned, a Sun-day assembly. But the further her eye strayed from this framework, the more endearing became the scenery, the grandeur dwindling through young offi-cials in shirt-sleeves and girl typists in mini-skirts, country boys in *loden*, round-armed waitresses and farm-girls in the *dirndl*, to a fringe of comfortable older women in working black and dark blue print, and children in very little of anything. The whole community was certainly represented. The carnival procession wasn't until this afternoon, half the town hadn't dressed for it yet, and still had work to do before it turned out on holiday.

She withdrew her eyes from the upper tiers, and took her place discreetly a step behind Lucas, as the worthies descended upon them with vast, hospitable smiles.

The central figure could be none other than Herr Graf, and it was easy to believe that most of the com-pulsive energy which had turned the pre-war summer fair into this ambitious tourist attraction stemmed from him, and at his instigation had generated the initiative which had brought Lucas Corinth home to his birthplace at last. Heinz-Otto Graf was a big man in austere but immaculate lightweight suiting, in a delicate shade of grey. He terminated everywhere in extremities rather surprisingly small for his central mass, moving lightly as a gazelle upon small feet, and gesturing vigorously with small hands. Even his head, round-faced, small-featured and closely trimmed as to its thick, iron-grey hair, looked at least one size small for him, though the bulging forehead promised a sizeable brain, and the fleshy but massive and jutting jaw an obstinate and assured will. Wherever he went, in however assertive a group, he would always be noticed first.

He bore down on Lucas with outstretched hand and a broad, victorious smile. 'Mr Corinth, may I welcome you home most warmly to Gries-am-See? I am Graf. I trust you had a pleasant journey?'

Lucas made the appropriate responses, and presented his daughter. From now on, Una realised as her hand was firmly grasped and ceremoniously kissed, she had to make use of the German she had certainly learned early from Lucas, but seldom used in recent years. No doubt someone who knew English would be in attendance on every occasion, just to be on the safe side, but some effort was also required from her. She acknowledged Graf's inevitable compliments cheerfully, and was complimented again on her pronunciation. He had a deep and not unpleasing voice, and sounded as happy with his captive lion as he looked.

'My wife, Frau Ottilie!'

She was a tall, willowy woman, dressed in an elegance slightly too formal for her shy manner and subdued and rather anxious face, and decidedly too warm for the day. She shook hands limply, and murmured monosyllables. They did well enough; clearly not much more was expected of her.

'And here is our art director, Werner Seligmann. Herr Seligmann has been rehearsing your work with the orchestra and soloists for two weeks now, I think you will find they already have a good basic conception of the piece.'

Lucas knew the name, as a sound and competent provincial conductor. He held out his hand to a thin, grey, elderly man with a clever, discouraged face and a hesitant smile. In Graf's vigorous shadow his attenuated shape and pale presence almost vanished.

'I look forward very much to reaping where you've been so kindly sowing for me. I hope,' said Lucas warmly, 'that you'll conduct the final performance yourself, and let me have the experience of hearing my music properly.'

'I hope you won't have to undo too much of what I've done,' said Seligmann, smiling. 'I must say you make great demands on your musicians.'

'I'm sure both you and they are quite equal to them.'

Lu was being a little too gracious, and committing himself a little too rashly, Una thought critically. The effort to be social cost him such an expenditure of energy that he was inclined to overdo it, and find himself launched into minor situations he had not intended. He'd be all right after one drink. And there were so many others waiting to be presented that he could hardly spend long enough with any one of them to get in too deeply. He was himself aware of his tendency, and always knew when he was overstepping, as a singer with true pitch knows when he is straining above the note, even if he can't therefore centre his voice and correct the fault.

Some of the names struck echoes in Lucas's ears. Some of the faces he could fit to the names, though it was a painful effort to grope his way back to the old days, and recall the families that had lived in Gries for generations. With some of these people he must have gone to school. He allowed himself to be steered up

the steps and into the building, Graf's short, powerful
hand firmly grasping his elbow.

'You would like to freshen up before our little
party. Oh, a very brief and modest affair, we know we
must not tire you out completely. Jörg will show you,
and bring you to the hall when you are ready. And
here may I present Fräulein Lohr, who will take care
of Miss Corinth. Fräulein Lohr speaks excellent
English – yes, I know it may sometimes be fatiguing
to continue always in German! – and she will be
attached simply to you during your stay, to arrange all
your appointments for you, have cars ready, take care
of your correspondence – everything! You will find
her very efficient. She is one of our best secretaries.'

The girl stood still and indifferent to be displayed to
them thus, and neither smiled nor frowned. His manner had not been at all condescending, merely practi-
cal, but rather as though he were recommending a
piece of office furniture than a person; and she kept
her face as placid and noncommittal as if she were
no more than that, though excellent of her kind. She
was several inches taller than Una, and probably six
or seven years older, a slender person in an unobtrusive dress of fine, creamy wool, sleeveless and simply
cut. She had not the ample build or the light-brown
colouring of most of the local women. The long,
smooth hair coiled on top of her head was almost
blue-black, and the eyes that seemed to fill half of her
oval face were of the same profound colour.

'I shall be very glad,' she said, looking neither
glad nor sorry, and in a voice cool and low and duti-
ful, 'to be useful to you in any way I can while you
stay here.'

Detailed off for the job, thought Una, as she went
away in Fräulein Lohr's correct company to wash off
the dust of travel, straighten her hair and the seams
of her stockings, and put on a new face. Maybe she's
had to postpone her own holiday, or something. Or
maybe she just doesn't want to presume on her selec-

tion for the job. For it seemed to her unlikely in the extreme that there could exist any girl who would not jump at the chance of being picked out to attend on Lucas. Not that proximity ever did any of them any good. He might notice a girl if she could sing like an angel, or play the harp like a seraph, but even then he wouldn't recognise her by her looks if he met her on the street.

'My name's Una,' she said briskly, smoothing powder over one tanned cheekbone. Begin as you mean to go on! 'What's yours?'

She could see the calm oval face in the mirror, and it was watching her with interest, but not as yet giving away anything of what went on behind it.

'You won't mind if we use first names? It's so much more friendly. And I hope this fortnight's going to be as pleasant for you as for us.'

'My first name,' said the girl accommodatingly, 'is Crista.'

'That's nice! It suits you.' And indeed she had a crystalline quality about her, her spareness, and polish, and that fastidious reserve that gave her so clear and pure an outline. 'I think it was a lovely idea to let us borrow you all the time we're here? Do you work here in the municipal offices usually?'

'I'm only here for the season. As a shorthand-typist in the festival office. Not the senior, but I happened to have the best English.'

They were speaking English, and she used it freely and almost without accent, apart from a precise attention to every consonant, and a reluctance to throw away syllables. For the first time she smiled. It was a very grave and thoughtful smile, but it softened every line of her face. 'I think everyone in the office volunteered. I was lucky to be chosen, I've been working here only a few months.'

'I'm awfully glad it was you. And I hope to make you just as glad, before we leave. There, I'm ready! I suppose we'd better go and circulate. Will you stay with me? I'm sure Herr Graf isn't going to let go of Lu for a moment, so *he* won't need you.'

The party proved, after all, quite surprisingly enjoyable, even if she had to work at it by attempting, for the first time in years, to think in German. In the great salon, heavy small-town baroque in white and tarnished gilt, its ornamentation oddly attractive and harmonious in spite of its honest crudity – or perhaps because of it – some fifty or sixty people circulated in comfort, nibbled voraciously at the light savouries and weighty sweets of a discreet buffet, too restrained to inhibit the solid lunches that would certainly follow, and drank, instead of sherry, a good Austrian white wine. And Crista Lohr, without visible reluctance or regret, hung attentively at Una's shoulder, furnished the names she omitted to memorise, prompted her when she fumbled for a word, saw that her glass stayed just sufficiently primed to discourage any ardent young man from refilling it, and steered her diplomatically away from the more boring encounters, on plausible grounds, after only a few moments.

As for Lu, he was surrounded three deep whenever she caught a glimpse of him. It was only to be expected, but it worried her, all the same. He had surely accepted this situation, with his eyes open, when he agreed to come here. Lions have to pay for being lions, he knew what he was inviting. If only he had a real skin, tough and elastic, like other men!

'At a quarter to one,' said Crista Lohr in her ear, softly and reassuringly, 'the car will be at the door for you, and I shall cut him out quietly from whoever is detaining him. It is part of my job,' she said, confronting the startled and almost daunted stare of Una's grey eyes, 'to protect the town's guest from every kind of pressure. We are only five minutes' drive from the Grand Hotel, where your reservations are made. At ten minutes to three I shall come back with the car to bring you here to see the carnival procession. Lunch is already ordered for you in your suite at the Grand, for one o'clock, and I hope you will have time to rest and relax before I come. This afternoon all you will have to do is watch, and listen, and take photographs.'

'Bliss!' said Una. 'That I can do with both hands tied behind me. He really does need a pause to breathe, you know. Coming back here was a terrific step for him to take. I don't know if you can understand that.'

'Yes,' said Crista simply, 'I can understand it. It has been a long time. The whole world has changed. There were stresses. And people do not always forget well enough.' She said, after a brief and thoughtful pause, in the same low and limpid voice: 'You are very fond of him.'

'He's my father,' said Una. And in sheer self-defence she said it with the hard, resigned lightness of the trapped young, acknowledging the debts they resent. For her it was a profanation and a lie, but she could not expose herself any more fearlessly than that.

'I understand,' said Crista politely. 'One does revere one's father. Naturally!'

CHAPTER TWO

The Grand Hotel was on the lake front, the windows of its best suites looking out over the Himmelsee towards the island. It was the only hotel in Gries with the slick, elaborated modernity of the postwar years, and though its design was solid and its whiteness inoffensive, it looked out of place after the narrow, intimate streets, and the gabled, iron-signed guest-houses. The only possible lodging for the son the town delighted to honour, though he would certainly have preferred any one of the stooping, comfortable inns he had known long ago.

He sat up stiffly at first sight of the glossy frontage. Crista's oddly-phrased comment had been, in its way, very accurate, Una reflected. *People do not always forget well enough.* Lu could not forget Gries as he had known it, and whatever defaced that image jarred and affronted his senses, underlining that he had become an alien.

'This is new,' he said, 'since my time.'

'It belongs,' said Crista from the front seat, without turning her head, and without any inflection that could be held to imply a comment, 'to Herr Graf.'

'Ahh!' he said in a sharp, understanding sigh. And after a moment of thought, reassembling this curve of the lake-shore as it had once been: 'There was a boat-house, and beyond, nothing but the fields, and inland the farm. This land belonged to the Sulzbachs. It was the very rim of the town.' It looked out now upon new villas, even a new street of shops, and a prolongation of the promenade.

'Herr Graf has bought up all this parcel of land, and more beyond. He is building another big hotel close to the castle. And the island, the Himmelhof – he has bought that, too. He is beginning to modernise it – oh, not to spoil the baroque quality, I mean to modernise with electric power and heating, and bathrooms. He will make that, too, into a luxury hotel. He says it could be as great an attraction as Isola Bella.' Her low, muted, deliberate voice avoided all coloration that could be interpreted as taking sides one way or the other. She reported scrupulously, and that was all.

Lucas said: 'I see!' in much the same tone, fastidiously aloof, refraining from judgment. Though of course he must be making his own assessments, how could he avoid it? One big new hotel functioning, two, including one superlative effort, in preparation. And the first ambitious July Festival already launched. And what else planned? Oh, yes, Gries-am-See was due to be placed on the tourist map in a very big way. It was not therefore necessary to conclude at once that Lucas Corinth was merely being employed as advertising matter. For all I know, Una thought, charitably and cheerfully, Heinz-Otto Graf genuinely loves music, and is busy combining all his interests to the general good of his town. In which case, good luck to him! The Grand Hotel was not, in fact, at all a bad effort, if he could keep up the standard.

The Mercedes drove into a pleasant, cool forecourt and crackled to a stop on golden gravel. Two small porters in *loden* came scurrying down white steps to take their luggage, and a shadowy foyer green with miniature trees and potted palms received them. Crista saw to everything, and did not leave them until they were installed in their lakeside suite, two bedrooms, bathroom and sitting-room, with a balcony over the water, with drinks and ice ready on a tray, and lunch on delivery at the touch of a bell.

'If there is anything that has been forgotten, please

ask at once, and it will be done. They have orders to meet all your wishes. At ten minutes to three,' she said punctiliously, 'I shall come with the car for you. It will be the opening procession, with music and dancers, and decorated floats, and we have places reserved for you on the mayor's balcony at the Town Hall. It will last perhaps an hour and a half. All the people from the fair will be there, too, the show men, the animals, the gypsies, the bands – I think you will like it.'

'I'm sure,' said Lucas, moved to painful personal consideration rather rare in him, 'that we shall like it very much.'

The girl withdrew in immaculate order, trim and self-contained from the rear view as from the front view, with a gait peculiarly proud and private, as though she reserved all her own personality immune from them. Lucas looked after her until she vanished beyond the white and gold door of the suite, his brows drawn together in a fretting frown that suggested headache. 'God!' he said, in a half-voice he used only to himself. 'How I need a drink!' He had made one and a half glasses of wine see him through all that benevolent minor hell, and the half-glass had been deposited intact when Crista had cut him out of the social whirlpool like a selected steer out of a herd. Very efficiently, no doubt about that. And he had been grateful to her. He *was* grateful.

Una drew the curtains wide, and stepped out over the shimmering water, which stretched away before her into the green folds of the hills. A lace of little white hotels fringing the green, all of them at least a hundred years older than this one, and a ladder of little blonde landing-stages prickling the blue. And half-withdrawn into the soft haze of the upper air, the sheer faces of the mountains. The Silvretta haunted this view, distant, brilliant and aloof, sky-diamonds.

There were flowers in their sitting-room, lunch appeared at the touch of a bell, and was well cooked and excellently served. There was every possible indication that Gries had made elaborate arrangements for the comfort of its prodigal son now that he had been lured home.

'All this,' said Una, glancing out from the window at the surrounding splendour, 'and VIP treatment, too! I always thought prophets weren't honoured in their own countries, but they've certainly rolled out the red carpet for you. Great man comes home! Welcome our wandering boy – a hero at eighteen and genius at forty-odd!'

'Stop talking nonsense!' said Lucas, with an unaccustomed snap of exasperation.

She turned in mild surprise, and gave him a long, narrow look, estimating the possibilities and finding them only moderately explosive. Lu could be temperamental at times, especially over music; and what with a big new work about to be launched on the world, and only an obscure provincial orchestra and soloists of unknown capabilities at his disposal for the purpose, he might well be on edge at this stage. After the first rehearsal he'd be all right. However inadequate his material – for she didn't quite believe in the optimistic estimates of Jörg-Erich and Herr Graf – he'd know then how to get the best out of it.

'Only half-nonsense to me, darling,' she said serenely, 'and not at all to them. Why shouldn't they think of you like that?'

Lucas stretched himself out full-length on the couch, with a resigned sigh. 'Heroes and geniuses are equally rare,' he said with lingering irritation, 'and I make no claim to be either, and never have, and I won't have you making it for me, either.'

'All right, no hero, no genius. But tell them, don't tell me.'

She glanced at the clock on the delicate, green-damasked wall. Nearly an hour before the car was due to collect them, and Lu still had the gift of prompt cat-napping and instant awaking that dated from the uneasy years of his boyhood here. His eyes had closed, he breathed long and softly, and his face had the distant calm of sleep already, but the tensions of his body had not relaxed. That was how he slept in times of stress, ready to be on his feet at any moment, and grasp instantly any situation to which he might open his eyes.

Una sat down in an armchair across the room from him, and studied him thoughtfully in the silence. The short brown hair paled into an edging of silver at his high temples. It had been like that as long as she could remember, and it only made him look more youthful than ever, echoing the greyness of his eyes, which her own so strongly resembled. After all, he was still barely middle-aged, only forty-seven, and built on a long, slender scale that would keep him looking active and elegant into old age. And with that thin face of his, those fastidious features and aloof eyes, he had always been a magnet to women, ever since Una's mother had died, nearly ten years ago. Una was used to that. At first she had guarded him like a small dragon minding a captive prince; but it had soon become clear that he needed no guarding from admiring females whom he never seemed even to see. These days, Una thought, she would almost be glad if he would catch sight of one of them, provided, of course, that he picked out one of the nicer ones. There was no denying he was a great responsibility.

Once, she remembered, in the first year of her total possession and greatest protective passion for him, she had had a stand-up fight with another girl at school, a real fight with torn dresses and pulled hair and scratched faces, because the other girl had bragged about her actor father until Una could bear it no longer, and had told her roundly who, of all the girls in England, had the handsomest father, the bravest and the most brilliant. The resultant uproar had sent her home in disgrace to collect a second lecture from the object of her adoration. She still remembered how superior it had made her feel to stand in silent forbearance, and let his anxious reproaches run off her like coronation oil. She never had told him what the fight was about, but some days later she had unbent so far as to inform him that she had won it.

She wouldn't have shared him with anyone, then; as he had become suddenly both father and mother to her, so she had assumed a like enlargement, and constituted herself everything her mother had been to him, hostess, secretary, manager, shock-absorber against the buffeting of a world not then quite so appreciative as it had since become. At ten years old, the surrender of any part of her absolute right in him would have meant the loss of her own personality. At twenty she looked a little further afield, and her world was peopled by a great many others besides Lucas, even if no one of them had yet come anywhere near supplanting him.

Meantime, she thought, eyeing the clock, I've just got nice time to unpack properly, and decide on a frock for tonight. Should she change for the afternoon? No need, she decided; after all, on this occasion they were only spectators, not playing a main part. But tonight she would have to pull out all the stops.

She was in her walk-in wardrobe, with a bouquet of dresses over her arm, and one hand operating as quietly as possible among the tinkling hangers, when the telephone rang in the sitting-room. She dropped the dresses on her bed, and ran to catch it before it could awaken Lu, but she should have known she would be too late. At the second ring he was already sitting upright and wide awake, his hand outstretched to pick up the receiver.

'Lucas Corinth here.'

Una heard the faintest of metallic murmurs at the other end of the line. Crista Lohr, perhaps, announcing her arrival for them from reception? No, there remained twenty minutes yet before she was due, and everything about her up to now suggested that she would arrive precisely when she had promised to arrive. Jörg-Erich, perhaps, with some detail that had been forgotten, or a slight change of timing? The possibilities, in this town where his family had been well known for generations, were wide and exciting, even, perhaps, to Lu himself, curiously alarming and discomfiting. Taking up links broken for nearly thirty years is a wincing business, no matter how much goodwill there is on both sides. She saw how the lines of his face had tightened and paled, and how still his body was, tensed as though he held his breath.

He did not speak again. He did open his lips, arduously, as though they had dried into parchment; but before he could utter a word she heard the infinitely distant and faint click of the receiver at the other end being replaced. The caller had simply spoken and hung up, without waiting for any reply.

Lucas replaced the handset with a movement very slow and careful, as though it weighed heavily in his hand. She saw him moisten his lips. Then he got up and crossed the room, his back turned to her, and helped himself to a cigarette from the box on the centre table. That was a mistake. The flickering of the match told her that his hand was shaking.

'What was it, Lu? Is there something wrong?'

A silly question, she thought. I know there's something wrong, and he knows I know it.

'Wrong? What should be wrong? Except the number,' he said, inhaling smoke, and turning upon her a face carefully composed, like a too exact portrait. 'They made a mistake at the switchboard downstairs. Someone was calling the next suite. She caught up with it next moment, and switched the call.'

If there was one thing Una was sure of, at that moment, it was that the entire staff of the Grand Hotel had been drilled into the fullest possible realisation of their duty to their guest of honour, and whatever room in this establishment received a mis-directed telephone call, it would not be the room Lucas Corinth occupied. It shocked her that he should lie to her, as by now it was probably shocking him that he could not make a more convincing job of it when the need arose. If he had to protect his privacy by lying it must mean that her very presence had been a trespass. She hadn't thought there was any ground at all where she could not confidently follow him. For the moment it was more unthinkable to force her way through the invisible barrier he had raised than to leave him to be wretched in loneliness on the other side of it.

This was one problem she had never faced before with her problem parent, and she didn't know how to deal with it; and her moment of indecision made it for ever impossible to say, as she might have said bluntly at once: 'I don't believe you! Now tell me the truth.'

'Oh!' she said flatly. 'I see! That was all.'

'That was all.'

But why should he turn his back again, unless it was because he didn't want her to see his face, or the hands that were still not quite steady?'

'Is that the time?' he said, looking up at the wall clock. 'I'd better go and wash, or the car will be here before I'm ready.'

He went away into his own room, and closed the door between them; and she had to stand and watch him go, infinitely farther than simply into the next room, and could think of no immediate way of draw-ing him back to her.

The procession took an hour and three-quarters to pass through the streets of Gries, from its gathering point on the fairground near the Filsertal woods. Installed in a place of honour on the balcony of the Town Hall, along with the official party, Una watched the cavalcade of decorated vehicles, tab-leaux, bands, dancers and singers wind its way unhurriedly round three sides of the square, and out again on its way back through the winding streets to its starting point.

The shock and preoccupation of that queer little scene with Lucas stayed with her only briefly. The sun shone too brightly, the holiday spirit was too insistent, to let her fret for long. And Crista at her shoulder, prompt and attentive, was ready with information on everything she wanted to know, from the origin of the banner of the town, borne at the head of the procession by a herald resplendent in local costume and mounted on a lively, russet-gold Haflinger, to the words of the song the smallest school-children were singing as their flower-filled wagon sailed slowly by under the balcony.

After the herald and his escort of horsemen came the town's brass band, and then the fantastic floats began, foaming with ribbons and flowers and balloons, and peopled by gnomes, giants, mermaids, Martians, monsters, princesses, dragons of fantasy and reality. Between the horse-drawn wagons came more bands, from villages lower down the valley, troops of dancers in local dress, individual carnival figures of every kind. Then a wave of excited laughter and cheering announced the approach of a small group of clowns and acrobats, and two spangled girls on horseback, and one glittering man in black tights who juggled coloured rings even as he walked.

'There's a circus here, too?' said Una, delighted. 'I didn't realise the festival cast its net so widely.'

'Oh, the circus has always come for the summer fair every year they are here. Didn't you see the tents and stalls from the road, when you came this morning? Out at the southern end of the town, where there's a big level meadow – that has always been the fairground. It's bigger than ever this year, the festival has attracted showmen from further afield, naturally, but all the old regulars will surely be there. Look, here are some of the gypsies.'

They came dancing, in a whirl of brilliant colours and blinding white smiles, to a ragged orchestra of their own. Ragged only in the casual disorder in which it marched, for its music had a frenzied precision. Their instruments were mainly strings, they walked with even the bass viols slung by leather straps from their shoulders, bowing unconcernedly, and fingering without any apparent need for concentration or thought. In the general merry uproar their music must have been practically inaudible to the musicians themselves, but it mounted clear of the shouting and laughter to reach the balcony in clear string tone, dazzlingly competent. In the tangle of show-ground folk that followed them some were gypsies, but many were not, and even among these latter there were a number of fiddlers and pipers. One tall, gaunt elderly violinist strode steadily ahead, playing with all his might, though he was led along by a little boy, who trotted beside him with a hand clasping the elbow of the arm that held the fiddle, and slowed or hastened his pace slightly according to the traffic around them, as though to preserve a clear space about his charge.

'He's blind!' said Una, suddenly realising the meaning of this partnership.

'Yes, I think you must be right.'

'Is he a regular, too? Everybody in the street seems to know him.'

'I expect he must be, but I don't know him. These wandering players usually make the same round of fairs and shows every season, and perhaps play in inns in the towns during the winter, or at family parties, weddings and christenings.'

'Not in orchestras?'

'Some may, of course. But most play by ear, they know no written music.'

The rising breeze that made the balloons dance brought back a distinct skirl of fiddle playing to Una's ears, momentarily clear of the gay hubbub of the street. A sparkling silver thread of sound. I only wish, she thought, astonished and charmed, that I could play like that. On any instrument – by ear or from the page!

'Then, too,' said Crista thoughtfully, 'most like better to play alone, and to be always moving on. And I think with country weddings, and fairs, and often free lodging, they make not a bad living.'

The procession, ending with a final resplendent float full of school-children, drew into its wash the entire population of the streets, which until now had stood crowded along the narrow pavements to watch. Now both hems of the crowd swirled outwards into the roadway and followed, laughing and singing, prolonging the pageant. Most of the town would spend the rest of the day on the fairground or by the lake. Shops and restaurants would do a brisk trade with the visitors from other regions and other countries, and the town brewery would dispose of prodigious quantities of beer, not much doubt of that. Una wondered, but did not ask, if Herr Graf had a controlling interest in the town brewery? It seemed more than likely.

The official party stirred gently out of its composed groupings on the balcony, circulated civilly for ten minutes or so to give everyone time to speak to the distinguished visitor, and adjourned to the salon to drink coffee before dispersing.

It was midnight when they got back to their suite at the Grand that night. Ordinarily Gries would have been fast asleep by that time, but now the town had adapted itself to the habits of its profitable guests, so that they had company in the lift, and could still hear dance music drifting up faintly from the garden on the lower terrace as they entered their sitting-room.

'Tired?' asked Lucas, his finger on the light switch.

'Not a bit. I should be asking you that,' she said wryly. 'Frau Graf is pretty heavy going, isn't she?' Her own partner at dinner had been, predictably,

Jörg-Erich Fischer – I wonder, she thought, if Jörg-Erich didn't make the table arrangements? – with Werner Seligmann on her other side, and she had found them both remarkably pleasant company. Especially after a glass or two of wine, which greatly assisted her fluency in German, she noticed. Lu must have needed quite a lot of wine to cope with Herr Graf's suppressed and monosyllabic consort. Not that he had drunk much tonight, or for that matter eaten much. She had been watching him from time to time, and she knew.

'Never mind, an easy day tomorrow,' she said consolingly. 'I thought we might even go and have a look at this fair. No social load there, nobody'd know us. Would you like me to ring for some coffee for you?' Sometimes, when he was tired almost to obliteration, it required a cup or two of strong coffee to restore him to a condition where he could fall asleep properly.

'No thanks, kitten. I shan't need it. I'm going straight to bed. Goodnight! Don't stay up too late.'

'I won't. Bathroom's all yours, I'd like mine in the morning. Goodnight, Lu!'

When the door of his room had closed on him, she went out through the parted curtains to the balcony, and looked out over the moony shimmer of the water, just barely quivering in the lightest of winds, and refracting into her eyes in infinitesimal sparks the distant starlight. Round the lake's rim the terrestrial lights glowed, indenting the live, liquid radiance with fixed stars. The air was mild, the darkness not dark, but milky with a lambent lustre. She felt as fresh as if she had risen from eight hours' sleep. And he looked worn to the bone and the essence, honed to a translucent fineness. It would be good for him to take her to the fair and ride all the crazy side-shows with her, and eat garish, indigestible sweets, and turn juvenile again at the circus. To forget himself for a day, and come back to himself quite fresh and new, seeing this whole relationship with his town from a different angle, and gloriously simplified. She was certain then that that was all he needed, and his hypersensitive dreads would all have fallen away from him. She knew him, after all, rather well.

Behind her, in the sitting-room, the telephone pealed abruptly. She turned with no foreboding in her mind, simply reacting to the summons as she would have done at home. The unpleasant impression left by the noontide incident was almost erased by this time, and she was afloat upon a philosophical tide laced with more wine than she normally allowed herself. She picked up the receiver with nothing in her mind but mild surprise at this late call, and a pleasurable curiosity about its motive.

The door of her father's room flew open abruptly, and there he was in his shirt-sleeves, confronting her across the table, his hand held out authoritatively to take the receiver from her. She almost handed it over with a shrug, she was so used to humouring him, and he had given her so little reason, ever, to resent any order or wish of his. But then, while the thing was still in her hand, she realised the importance of what she was doing. She looked Lucas squarely in the eye, and put the receiver to her ear.

'Yes? Lucas Corinth here!'

CHAPTER THREE

She had tuned her voice as low as she could, to a brusque and muted murmur, but the listener at the other end knew.

'Miss Corinth?' said a husky whisper in her ear, in German. 'Will you be so kind as to give your father a message from my father, please? The name is Gelder, Valentine Gelder. Will you say that my father expects him during the next few days? Say he is looking forward to the meeting.'

'Why of course!' she began, relaxing into relief and pleasure at a message so innocuous. 'He is here himself now. Would you like to . . .' She broke off there, as the small, final sound of the distant receiver being replaced stabbed at her senses again like an ominous pinprick of mistrust. Why the whisper? Or was she imagining it? Why the haste to get off the line? She looked up at Lucas over the mute instrument, and slowly laid it in its cradle.

'He rang off. He didn't wait. But it's only somebody who seems to be hoping for a visit from you, Lu. I bet there are a lot of people here who used to know you, and are hoping to meet you again.'

She heard the strained tone in her own voice, and wondered whom she was trying to convince, herself or him. He was very pale, but his voice was quiet and calm.

'Well, who was it? What did he have to say?'

She told him, word for word, hoping for an easing of the white tension in his face, a sign that he had been nerving himself needlessly for some other and less

33

innocuous message. He lowered his eyes to evade hers, and went on carefully extracting the thin gold links from his cuffs; but if anything the pale, hard lines that outlined his features whitened still more distressingly.

'You're sure of the name?' He was quiet and calm. 'It was Gelder?'

'Valentine Gelder. He said he was speaking for his father.' She no longer expected the thing to go away in peace. It was there between them, invisible but palpable, and there was no longer any point in pretending that there had been anything normal about that call, or concealing any of the disquieting details of it. 'There was something odd about him,' she said. 'He was whispering. And as soon as I began to answer he rang off.'

'It's late,' said Lucas reasonably. 'I expect he was in a hurry because he felt he was keeping us up. He's probably tried several times for us, earlier in the evening.'

'Do you know them, these Gelders?'

He hesitated for a fraction of a second, and turned a little away from her as he said: 'Not the son. I knew the father very well.'

'Were you expecting to hear from him?'

This time she saw the thin cheek nearest her contract in what might have been a convulsive smile. 'No,' he said at last, 'not particularly. There are lots of people who may take the trouble to get in touch, of course, but I can't say I was expecting Gelder.'

'Well . . . shall you visit him, then?'

He raised his eyes for an instant to her face, and said: 'Quite probably. We shall see.' He had himself well in hand now, he could face her and smile at her, even venture himself within her reach. He leaned and kissed her forehead. 'Go to bed, love! Good night!'

He marched towards the door of his room; he was going, just like before, and leaving the frontier closed against her, and if he got away from her now she would feel that she had lost him completely. She ran indignantly, and put her back against the door, and held him before her by the shoulders. He felt cool and hard and smooth through the thin shirt, like an athletic boy. He tried to look surprised and indulgent, but it wasn't a complete success.

'No, you don't!' she said with determination. 'Who do you think you're talking to, anyhow? Do you think I can't tell when you're telling me lies?'

'I thought it was wives who were clairvoyant about that, not daughters,' he said, ruefully smiling.

'Lu, *don't*! This isn't any joke, and you know it. That call this afternoon was from the same man, wasn't it? There's something wrong about all this, terribly wrong, and I want to know what it is. If there's something troubling you it troubles me, too, surely you know that?'

'You're being silly,' he said. 'Nothing whatever is wrong, nothing's troubling me, except what sort of collection of local band parts they've swept together for me. And if you're going to bully me I shall wish I'd left you at home. There, scat!'

'No. It's no good, Lu, you can't get away with that. You can't treat me like a contemporary until I'm grown up, and then suddenly shut me out. Unless, of course,' she said warmly, herself beginning to be angry, 'we only were contemporaries until I grew up. If that's the way you want me to think of you, you're going the right way about it.'

That brought him up short against a picture of himself which he didn't like at all; it even brought a slight flush to his pale face. Perhaps there was too much truth in it for it to be comfortable hearing, even if she herself didn't believe in what she had said. After a moment a faint and reluctant smile softened the bleak lines of his mouth.

'Am I really behaving so childishly?'

'Yes,' she said firmly. 'After living with me as long as you have, you ought to know there's nothing you

THE HORN OF ROLAND

can't share with me. There's nothing I wouldn't offer *you* a share in. Bad or good!'

'That's what you think! Wait a little while, there will be!' But he couldn't hold out against her. He stood looking down at her ruefully, torn two ways. 'If I tell you, you may wish I hadn't. And I may wish it, too.'

'I never shall. And I won't let you, either. Do you think anything could be as bad for me as your not trusting me?'

'I shouldn't have brought you here,' he said helplessly. 'I should never have come. And yet it had to happen, sooner or later. It might as well be now. I couldn't have kept away for ever.'

'You'd better tell me,' she said reasonably, sure of herself now. He had come too far to turn back and go through all that effort of disentanglement and denial again. 'Come and sit down here, and tell me. Wait a minute, I'll bring your dressing-gown.'

She closed the windows, too, on her way back with it. Who knew what kind of secret they might not be exposing to the vulnerable medium of words? She sat down on the rug, close to his chair but not touching him, because she felt so sharply in her own flesh how little he wanted to be touched just then. It wasn't easy for him; his skin was thin enough at the best of times, the brushing of a hand now might be agony to him. Even this hitherto safe and relatively simple relationship, it seemed, was fraught with all kinds of complex perils of hypersensitivity and misunderstanding. The price of love is always constant vigilance, constant and mature consideration. There aren't any easy loves; you have to work at it life-long.

'This is going back a long time,' said Lucas, staring into the smoke of his cigarette.

She knew that; it had to be something that had happened here, before ever he escaped from Gries. But she said nothing, only waited for him to find the words he wanted. She felt no alarm now; only his withdrawal from her had dismayed her. It was quite impossible that he could have anything to tell her that reflected discredit upon himself, and now that the crisis was passing she expected nothing worse – though that could be dangerous enough – than some recollection distorted by his over-tender conscience, and fed by time from a triviality into a monstrosity.

'You know how I left here, in the summer of 1944. Two of us got over into Switzerland that night, Helmut Vogel and me. What you don't know,' he said, 'is that there should have been three of us, if everything had gone according to plan.'

He had never talked willingly about those war years, when he was a boy here just working his way through the gymnasium. She knew the bare bones that were known to everyone: that in this valley, where the mountain barrier along the frontier was passable in several places to men born and bred here, there had existed the final cell of an underground organisation which had spirited away into Switzerland nearly a hundred anti-Nazi fugitives before it was penetrated and broken. She had traced in the distance, this morning, the beginning of the route, until it lost itself in the twisted folds of the Filsertal. She knew that Lu had graduated from school into the risky profession of guide, and taken part in many of those nocturnal expeditions, including the last, when the organisation was already shattered, and many of its key figures in custody or on the run. He had never gone into detail, had answered questions only grudgingly and briefly. That had never puzzled or disquieted her; that was his nature. There was even a degree of guilt in his unwillingness to discuss it; however much he had contributed, he would inevitably have found it falling short of what he owed. Also, the habit of reticence was all that had preserved the group for so long, and he had maintained it instinctively afterwards. Even now he was having to drive out every word over the barrier of his own reluctance.

'He was seventeen years older than I, a foreman at the saw-mill down by the river. I'd been working under his orders for three years, it was he who recruited me. That year things were getting too hot for comfort, and in July we got word that our contacts inland were being picked off one by one, and the net was out for us. It was one of our own friends on the run who brought us word, and we had him hidden in the hay-huts up on the alm until we could get him over the frontier. By then we knew that we should have to get out ourselves, and that we couldn't hope to have more than two or three days to do it.'

He sat silent for a moment, peering back, under painfully drawn brows, into a past which came to terrifying life again as soon as words, like blood, were fed into its veins.

'Our work had become difficult and complicated some time before that because, having failed to stop all the gaps by official means, the provincial police had started a new security group, and had armed plain-clothes patrols out by night along the frontier. Not local men, because it would have been difficult to keep their identities from leaking out. But we had an agent who had infiltrated the group, and supplied us with all the information we needed, got us samples of their identification cards, even stole some of their small arms for us. They couldn't cover the whole frontier, but we never could be sure where they would be at any given time, and our only safe way was to provide the men we smuggled out with documents like theirs, in case they were stopped somewhere. We had an engraver in Innsbruck, an artist, who provided these faked papers for us, complete with photographs, like enough to pass our men out, but not to identify them if wanted posters were out for them. He needed to be an artist! This time he had to prepare the same papers for us, and in a hurry. We agreed there was nothing else to be done. For the three of us. For Helmut Vogel. And me. And Valentine Gelder.'

'Not Valentin?'

'His mother was English, he was christened with the English name. He was married,' said Lucas, his lips tightening painfully. 'He'd been married nearly two years. His wife was expecting her first baby. She wasn't from here, he married her in Linz, and her people were still there. He wanted her to go back to them after he was gone. His name had become a danger to her in Gries. The day we were to go I had to sneak out of Gries and drive to Innsbruck on a borrowed motor-bike, as soon as it was dusk, to fetch the papers, while Valentine made the last dispositions for his wife. I was to meet him with the documents at the gate that crosses the track at the opening of the Filsertal, at eleven o'clock that night. By then it would be fully dark, and beyond the fairground the woods give good cover round the gate. The summer fair was in town, just as it is now, and the circus, all the usual booths and side-shows – noise enough and movement enough to help us, and plenty of drunks to occupy the local police.'

She saw again the bowl of the lake outlined beneath her as she had seen it that morning. Coming from Innsbruck and Landeck, he would have the whole of the town – though far smaller than it was now – between himself and the Filsertal gate.

'I got back into the town in plenty of time. I put away the bike, and started working my way out towards the edge of town. And I found a cordon of police drawn all round that side of Gries, encircling the fairground and the woods. They weren't our local men, they'd been brought in for the job, and there were SS men with them. I tried working my way round by the fields to get through them at a different point, or round them, but they were everywhere. I thought perhaps if I lay up somewhere and waited they'd be withdrawn. After all, it might not be us they were after. And I was early, I could afford an hour at least. But I waited an hour, and they didn't either move away or close in. I was outside the cordon there, I could have got away safely to join Helmut at the hut on the alm, but I couldn't go and leave Valentine. I tried to get through the line, down towards the gate, but I couldn't finish it, they were too many and too close. I was frightened sick, I couldn't do it. Eleven o'clock passed, and half past eleven, and midnight, and then suddenly there was a stir, and word passed along the line, and they drew off and went back into the town. No more stealth, I heard them passing the order along. Whatever they were there for had either been completed or abandoned. And I was free to go down to the meeting-place. I won't pretend I liked doing it. I didn't know whether some of them were still left in ambush, and the rest withdrawn expressly to fool me. I didn't know where Valentine was, or what had been happening there. All the fairground was dark and silent, everybody'd gone to earth, no organs, no one stirring. I was more afraid than I've ever been in my life. But I went down along the edge of the woods to the gate.

'He wasn't there. I worked my way along among the trees on either side, and I nearly walked into a man standing motionless in the darkness against one of the trunks. Stark still, like a tree himself. Not one of *them*. I had a nose for them, and for those who were hiding from them, too, and I knew which this fellow was. He'd been listening to me moving cautiously around for some time, and never moved a muscle in case I was on the other side. I don't know whether I really believed it was Valentine, or whether I only desperately wanted it to be, but I forgot about caution, and cried out aloud to him: Valentine, thank God! And then he moved and drew breath. I'd been right about him, he'd frozen there in the bushes for fear I might be one of the hunters. But wrong about everything else. I didn't know him. An older man, I thought maybe around forty, with a sack under his arm, or something rolled in sacking, and a smell and a shape about him that went with the fairground. I think if he'd belonged to Gries I should have known him, even in the dark. He came out of his thicket. We couldn't see much of each other, but I could smell fear on him, and surely he could on me, and that made us allies. A big, tall, rangy fellow with a bronchial voice. He asked me who I was looking for, and I told him. He said he'd been stuck in the woods there over an hour, like me, and couldn't even get away from the gate again because the cordon was drawn so tightly there. He said some time after eleven o'clock he'd heard them corner a man who came out of the woods on the town side, and overpower him and take him away. He didn't know his voice, but he heard his name pass, and heard him admit to it. They've got him, he said, and they left the cordon out an hour after that, waiting for somebody else, but nobody came. And the best thing you can do, he said, if you're the somebody, is get out of here quickly. You won't see him again. Not alive.'

His voice was calm, quiet and very tired. This story which she had never heard before had been repeated over and over, scrupulously, within his mind, until every word in it was chosen and final. The definitive version.

'And that's what I did. There was Helmut waiting up on the alm, and I had his papers, too, and he, at least, could be got out alive, with any luck. He didn't know the region as I did, he needed me to see him over the border. But still there might – there *might*! be a chance of escape, or rescue, for Valentine, and if a miracle happened the legitimation I had in his assumed name might be useful yet. I didn't dare wait and go back into town with it. And I had nobody to trust with it except this man I didn't even know. I took a chance on him. I gave him the card that was for Valentine, and asked him to deliver it to Willi

Bruchmann at the saw-mill. He was Valentine's deputy there, and as far as we knew then his cover hadn't been blown. If there was any chance at all, he was the man to make the most of it. And my man promised he would do it. Maybe I could have done better, somehow, I don't know how. Then it seemed the only thing to do.

'And I set off up the Filsertal to the alm, and I took Helmut over the border. We didn't have it easy all the way. Before the pass we ran into an official SS patrol, and had to show our faked papers, but we were lucky. They took us at face value and let us through. We got safely over into Switzerland. And Valentine – I didn't hear anything certain about him until after the war, when one of the Engelharts came over to England.'

'They killed him?' asked Una in a very low voice.

'Shot him. After a week of trying to get information out of him, and getting none. After the execution, Engelhart told me, Ina Gelder left Gries. I suppose she went back to her family. She never came back here, and where she bore her baby I don't know. But it's pretty clear now that she taught him to hate me, and to lay his father's death at my door.'

'Did he tell you that, too? – this Engelhart? That that was how she saw it? Lu, you haven't had this on your mind all this while, and never said a word to me?'

'No!' he said vehemently. 'I tell you she vanished from Gries and never came back. Good God, no! Don't you think if I'd known I should have done something about finding her, and getting the record straight? No, it was left for her son to tell me that. He must have been waiting a long time for me to come back to Gries.'

'And that was the son I spoke to?' She raised appalled eyes to her father's face. 'But he said: *"My father's expecting you . . ."*' Her voice foundered. The implications were too terrible to be put into words.

'He said what he meant,' said Lucas, and with neat, economical movements ground out his cigarette in the ash-tray. 'The words were carefully chosen.'

'And that first call, this afternoon – that was him, too, wasn't it? What did he say to you?'

'The first message was equally to the point. He said: "You've been a very long time coming to the meeting-place, Mr Corinth. My father had to go on ahead, but he's waiting for you just along the road. I'll let him know you're coming." '

'But it's crazy!' she protested furiously. 'You *did* go to the meeting-place. Why didn't you explain? You weren't to blame, why didn't you tell him so?'

'He didn't wait to let me tell him anything. And even if I did tell him, what reason has he to accept my word? Obviously he's always been led to believe that I took to my heels over the pass at the first sign of trouble, and left Valentine to wait for me at the gate until the SS came to collect him. And what proof can I offer that I ever came to the rendezvous? Nobody belonging to the town saw me or spoke to me that night. The man I did talk to wouldn't even know my name, and within a week or so he'd be gone from the town. He may be dead long ago. There's just my word for it that I ever came. I doubt if that would carry much conviction with a boy who's been taught almost from birth that I left his father to die.'

'There was Helmut,' said Una eagerly. 'The man who was waiting for you at the hay-huts. You must have told him what had happened. He could bear out the timing – and that you told the same story then.'

Lucas smiled, faintly and sadly. 'Helmut was sixty years old when we left. He's been dead now for nearly fourteen years.'

'But there must be something we can do,' she persisted fiercely. 'Don't you see what this means? He's threatening your life! Lu, you've got to tell the police about these telephone calls.'

He shook his head very decidedly. 'No, I can't do that.'

'But why not? You must! It's your life, Lu. In the next few days, he said . . .'

'It was Valentine's life, too. This issue between us is a life.'

'But you didn't kill him,' she protested helplessly. 'What could you have done? They'd taken him. If you'd stayed you'd have died, too, and so would Helmut, but you still wouldn't have been able to save Valentine. You couldn't have hoped to. If he could have spoken to you then, I bet he'd have said: Go on, get out of here, quickly!'

Lucas jerked his head aside with a motion of such pain that she shrank from touching him, and drew back a step in deference to his private anguish. 'I daresay he would. But we're not necessarily justified in taking everything the generous hold out to us. Maybe I couldn't have done any good, maybe it would only have been two deaths instead of one. But how do I know? I didn't try. Surely there was some way I could have got through the cordon before eleven, and warned him off. Or at least tried! Surely at the worst I could have waited to see if I could help his wife. Oh, of course I had to get Helmut over the frontier, but did I therefore have to cross with him? I could have come back. If I'd been the man he was I might even have found a way of rescuing him. Sometimes it succeeded, once in a thousand tries. How do I know, how can I ever know now, that this might not have been the thousandth time? No, whatever I do I can never get free of it. The boy may be mistaken in thinking what he does, but all the same, he has just cause for complaint against me. The issue's between us two. I won't bring the law into it.'

'But, darling, if you don't do something to defend yourself he'll kill you! Everything you're saying is nonsense. There was absolutely nothing you could have done. They were already hunting for you. If you'd set foot inside the town again you'd have been pitched straight into prison with him, and you know it. It's ridiculous and – and *arrogant*! – to demand miracles of yourself – not honourable. And if you don't tell the police, I will.'

But she knew she wouldn't, and by the pale smile that twitched at his lips, so did he. She couldn't go against his will, not even to save his life, and that not out of any awe of him or abdication of her own personality, but because such a failure in comprehension might do him worse damage than the threat from outside. The tortuous conscience of his was too vulnerable, too subject to self-torture and self-reproach, for her to risk hurting it even for the sake of keeping his body unhurt. She closed her eyes upon starting tears of frustration and anger.

'You're hopeless! You don't owe him anything at all. I suppose you're so damned stubborn that if anybody's going to die, this time, you're going to make absolutely sure it's Lucas Corinth! Just to satisfy your own impossible ideas of yourself! And what about me?'

That was hitting low, but the shock did him good. And it was surely a useful diversion to hack a morsel of guilt out of his inexhaustible supply upon a new and near pretext.

'I'm sorry!' he said, stung and ashamed. 'I'm letting my judgement be distorted out of all reason. Look, we're making far too much of this whole thing. Intense young men threaten what they never intend to do, and even if they do intend to act, they're not always very competent in performance. Nothing has happened yet, and probably nothing will. If I could meet the boy and talk to him we might understand each other very well. But I can't just turn the police loose after him. How much I contributed to Valentine's death I don't know, but I'm not going to make any mistakes with his son.'

'There are things *we* could do,' she insisted resolutely. 'There's this man Bruchmann at the saw-mill – even if he isn't there any more, maybe we could trace him. If he received Valentine's papers, that would be confirmation. He wouldn't have forgotten, even in all this time. We could make inquiries about Mrs Gelder, and try to contact her and her son. The one thing we can't do is sit passively waiting for someone to take a pot shot at you from a dark doorway, or toss a bomb in at the window here.'

He wanted to say: It won't be like that. He must be his father's son, he has nothing against you, and me he means to meet face to face. But he had the wit to hold his tongue, apart from accepting her energetic suggestions with slightly deceitful agreement, and promising everything possible to find young Gelder and bring him to reason.

'Tomorrow – yes, we shall see our way more clearly after we've slept on it. Nothing will happen. If we hadn't been tired and excited we should hardly have believed in it tonight . . .'

Over her head his eyes levelled into the darkness outside the window a composed and resigned stare. *And what about me?* An apposite question! He was glad he had left all his affairs in order. Una would be left well provided for. Tomorrow he would draft a letter to his solicitor, to clear up whatever trailing ends remained. Probably a needless precaution, of course; all that he was saying to her now about barking dogs who never bite might very well be true. Still, it was well to be ready.

CHAPTER FOUR

Crista Lohr presented herself next morning, as soon as they had breakfasted, tapping rather shyly at the door of their suite with her briefcase under her arm. She was at Mr Corinth's disposal for the whole of his visit. If he had letters to type, business arrangements to make, engagements locally to fit in between his official appearances, or if Miss Corinth wished to make some excursions when he was otherwise engaged, Miss Lohr would be happy to take care of everything. And as he had preferred not to have a rigid programme made for him in advance, she had thought it best to come early this morning, and find out if he had any special wishes for the coming days, so that she could be sure of laying on cars and tickets as required.

'Perhaps,' said Lucas, drawing up a chair to the table for her, 'we should go through the rehearsal schedule first, and then we shall know just what time we have left in between.'

She put on a pair of austere, dark-rimmed spectacles, and bent earnestly over her folio of official engagements. And Lucas sat down beside her, and gave his mind to the business for which he had come to Gries-am-See. Whatever happened, music at least deserved to be treated with respect.

'The première is one week from tomorrow, as you know. The first orchestra rehearsal is arranged for tomorrow afternoon, and of course I shall bring a car for you. The following morning we have tentatively fixed for a full rehearsal with the soloists, but you may prefer to meet them first separately for a piano rehearsal. There is a suitable room for that, too, with a good piano. If you approve this further schedule of rehearsals, in principle, they can always be altered as the need arises. Further sessions can be added if you find it desirable.'

She laid the neatly typed list before him.

'If all goes well,' said Lucas remotely, half his mind distracted by a sudden conviction of the outrageous acceleration of time rushing past him and out of his grasp, 'this will do splendidly. I am terrified of over-rehearsing. If a point needs labouring, it has not been well made in the first place. After tomorrow's session I shall be able to tell you exactly what I require. And hopefully, these arrangements will be perfectly adequate.'

'Good! Then there are a few functions at which we hope you will like to be present. The town has planned an al fresco lunch in the private garden of the castle for the day after the première. We hope the weather will remain reliable, but if not, there is one very beautiful old room inside which is still rainproof, it will be held there. And the other "must" is the final ball with which the festival ends. It will be a carnival affair, fancy dress if you would like to indulge. For Miss Corinth I can arrange a costume, perhaps traditional local dress? It can be very beautiful, especially at its most elaborate, and it would be a present from the town. They would like to think she may wear it at home for just such balls.'

Una, out on the balcony in a lounge chair of quilted floral plastic, heard half of this, but chose to remain apart from it. She needed room and time to think, for if anyone was to set the wheels of enquiry turning, she suspected it would have to be herself. Crista, however agreeable, however discreet, was an interloper here at this moment.

Yet she watched them, from the white blaze of sunshine over the lake, with wondering appreciation, seeing them cool and dim and dreamlike, there in the silvery-green shade of the room. Two slender, tall, rather beautiful people, equally earnest and devoted. Lu looking incredibly young in slacks and sports shirt, turning the pages of his diary and making notes with those nervous, immaculate movements of his long hands, as if everything he touched had life, and must be handled with delicacy; and the girl Crista very trim and prim in yellow linen, with smooth black hair drawn up into a soft coil on top of her head, and deep, rich colour ebbing and glowing in her oval face at the great man's nearness. Oh, she was very much aware of him! Women always were, and not all of them got as close as this. Her colour was a tide respondent to his words and looks and mild, abstracted attentions, and her voice, however severely controlled, quivered with sensibility at every unconsciously flattering modulation of his. She had a low-pitched voice, self-effacing but vulnerable, and a concentrated gravity beyond her years. She couldn't possibly be as much as thirty, quite probably no more than twenty-five or -six, but by the air of efficiency that clung about her she must have been at this job for several years. She had fine hands, too, strong, shapely, expressive, for use, not for a cosmetician's show-case. Una thought how lucky they had been. The office linguist might so easily have been middle-aged, voluble and thrusting, everything Crista Lohr was not. It would be no hardship to be escorted about the Tyrol by this attractive contemporary. Except, of course, that she had no intention, as things had turned out, of going a step away from Lu's side, even at rehearsals, where he would certainly think her a confounded nuisance. That didn't matter. She couldn't let him out of her sight now.

'And now,' said Crista, pleased, shuffling one batch of papers back into her briefcase and flattening a notebook before her at the ready, 'there must be something I can arrange for you today, before the serious work begins. Also you may wish to contact certain old friends here? And Miss Corinth did mention that she would like to go to the fair one day, and perhaps the circus.'

'It might be a very good idea,' Lucas said, 'for you to take her there this afternoon, if you're free. I ought to have a long session with Herr Seligmann, myself, before we begin work in earnest. And yes, there are some people I should very much like to see again, if it's possible. After so long without communication, one is rather hesitant – So many things could have happened in the meantime. There is a man who used to be employed at the saw-mill . . . It still belongs to the same company?'

'Metzler and Schmidt. I think it has always been Metzler and Schmidt?'

'Yes, that's the same firm. There was a man who knew my family quite well – if he's still with them after all this time. His name is Bruchmann – Willi Bruchmann.'

Una sat still in the sunlight, listening with relief and gratitude. He really meant to mend his defences, to begin mustering the evidences of his integrity. Even his reservation of the afternoon, which at first she had been inclined to challenge and dispute, might at this rate mean a session in the town archives rather than a musical discussion with Werner Seligmann. She had better give him his head, even if it meant trusting him to others for a few hours.

'Would you like me to call the mill for you, and get Mr Bruchmann on the line?'

The brief pause before Lucas answered sharply pointed the difference between Crista's simple secretarial view of such a transaction, and the headlong dive back into the past which it constituted for him. But when he spoke it was to say with composure: 'Would you be so kind?'

Difficult to envisage from that calm tone the inward convulsion of effort it cost him, like heaving up the slabs that covered long-accustomed and long-respected graves.

Una heard the number dialled. In the interval before the distant end answered she heard the very soft, gentle lapping of the lake-water under the balcony, patting the steps of the terrace.

'Good morning! Would it be possible for me to speak with Herr Bruchmann, please? Bruchmann, Willi. Oh! – yes, I see. Yes, it was some years ago that he was with the company. Perhaps Herr Metzler would know how we can get in touch with him now. Be so kind!' Crista looked over the receiver at Lucas, and said doubtfully: 'There is no one of that name employed at the mill now, or for some time back. But I spoke only with the reception clerk, the manager may be able to tell us where we can find him.'

'He may very well be retired,' said Lucas. 'He must be well into his sixties by now.'

'But they will know if he is still living in Gries.' She turned back alertly to the telephone. 'Herr Metzler? I was enquiring about a Willi Bruchmann, who used to work for you – for your company,' she amended, almost palpably reckoning the years since Lucas had left, and realising that this same Metzler was barely fifty. 'It would be more than twenty-five years ago.'

'Twenty-eight,' said Lucas automatically.

'Twenty-eight years, I am told. I am enquiring for a friend who has lost contact with him since then, and would like to get in touch again if possible. If you could, go so far back in your books . . .' She was silent for a moment, while the telephone clacked briskly and without pause in her ear. 'You do remember him? Then . . .' This time the pause was much longer. 'No, I didn't know. Yes, as you say, it's a very long time ago. Yes, I'm sorry, too. Thank you! I'm sorry to have troubled you.'

She cradled the telephone slowly. Una had left her place on the balcony, and stood mute and uneasy between the curtains.

'I'm sorry, it is not good news. I'm afraid it won't be possible to put you in touch with Mr Bruchmann.'

'He's dead,' said Lucas with flat certainty, and braced his shoulders under a small added weight. 'In twenty-eight years,' he said ruefully, 'so many people must have died. I don't know why I should have expected . . . But sixty isn't old!'

'It was not like that,' said Crista. 'Herr Metzler told me . . . He died very long ago. The SS took him away from his home, that night they came to the town in July of 1944. He never came back. He died somewhere in a concentration camp in Germany.'

Una saw Lucas's long hand flatten itself into white-knuckled rigidity on the table before him. They had indeed been busy prising up the slab of a grave.

They were still facing each other with still features and shadowed eyes across the table when the telephone rang, a loud, jangling sound that made them both start. They reached for the receiver together, Lucas with a nervous vehemence that told Una plainly what he expected now of any call that was put through into this room. But Crista was nearer, and reached the instrument before him. She was there to take upon herself all his secretarial work, and she took her duty seriously.

'You permit?'

'Please!' he said, and drew back and left it to her. Perhaps he was even glad to have the thing taken out of his hands. If it was the whisperer again the matter would no longer be secret, it would end with the police being called in in spite of him. But no, this was daylight and normality.

'Herr Graf is below,' said Crista, turning a slightly doubtful and concerned face upon Lucas, 'and would like to come up and see you. I don't know . . . He seems to be upset about something. He says it is urgent.'

'Please ask him to come up,' said Lucas. As far as he was concerned, at this moment Heinz-Otto Graf was an anti-climax, even on urgent business and in an excited state. He was positively welcome, with his minor annoyance – for what could be on his mind but some hitch in his imperial plans? – as a counter-irritant just when one was needed. The invasion of the everyday was steadying and reassuring.

The most perfunctory of taps at the door hardly preceded the entry of Herr Graf. He erupted into the room in a gust of agitated air, his broad-brimmed grey hat in one hand, a disintegrating newspaper in the other. The tough, round, cleanshaven face was russet, the big shoulders thrust through the air as though he were forcing his way irritably through a crowd. Light and formidable on his small feet, he loomed across the silver-green carpet and pulled up abruptly with his solid thighs against the edge of the table. Upset seemed a mild word for his condition. Frantic would have been nearer the mark, though his control was still absolute. Lucas, who had risen to meet him, was struck silent with astonishment at the sight of him.

'I apologise for intruding upon your rest day like this, Corinth, but this is an emergency. If I had had the least idea that anything of this kind could possibly crop up . . . It is terrible . . . outrageous! We cannot let it go unanswered, you must see that. I demand that you take some action to counter it, immediately, otherwise the effect upon the festival – upon the town – will be disastrous. There's not an hour to be lost. We have too much at stake . . .'

It was never very safe to say 'I demand' to Lucas, in that or any other tone. Una saw his lips and nostrils whiten with threatening resentment, and then the faint, grey shadow of uncertainty, of haunting doubt, took the icy edge from his features. In a chilly but reasonable voice he said: 'My dear Graf, I'm afraid I simply don't know what you're talking about. Whatever it is, I'm sure something can be done about it. I am as concerned with the success of the festival as you are. Why don't you sit down and tell me what's on your mind? For I assure you I haven't so far the least idea.'

But he had! Already he had. No very clear idea as yet, but a perception, at least, of the hand of his enemy. If one party in the duel could begin marshalling his forces and planning his moves, so could the other. And if one withheld his hand from attacking in public out of a morbid but characteristic tenderness of conscience, the like punctilio was not necessarily to be expected of the other.

'You mean you really don't know? No one has mentioned . . . ? Don't you read the papers?' It was incredible to him that there should be anyone who did not read the papers.

'Very seldom,' said Lucas, and glanced involuntarily at the small table by the door, where the folded newspapers still lay untouched.

'Then read now. See what this rag blazons across the front page!' Even in this disturbing moment Una could not help reflecting that the *Zeitung* must be one of the few things in Gries in which Heinz-Otto Graf did not own a controlling interest. A small, smooth fist brandished the offending paper before Lucas's eyes, and slapped it down upon the table in front of him. But in his agitation Graf made such heavy weather of refolding the sheets to display the front page that for a few moments it was impossible to read anything. 'Yes, read it for yourself! See what kind of story someone is casting up against us, and then consider what it can mean to me. After the most ambitious plans ever conceived here! On the day after the opening – this! Do you wonder I'm upset?'

Una stole silently across the room to her father's side. The aggressive motion of the heavy head towards him, thrusting like a bull, the very tone of the indignant voice, seemed to be accusing him of some act of sabotage. Between the blunt, enraged hands that smoothed the front page she caught a glimpse of a banner headline, of Lu's name, and a large, clear photograph. Something about a letter, received unmailed at the editorial office – signed . . .

Signed Valentine Gelder. And Lucas, with drawn brows and motionless face, was reading it, with deliberation now, from beginning to end.

Una walked unregarded and in silence round the table and the two men who confronted each other across it, crossed the room, and took up the virgin *Zeitung* that still lay in its crisp, flat folds on the side table. She read as Lucas read. She had to know the whole of it, the worst that hung over them.

'LUCAS CORINTH BETRAYED MY FATHER,' said the headline, prudently qualifying the assertion in smaller print with: 'says Son', but making its point as violently as possible from the outset. She could read German reasonably well, and the meaning of the whole, jettisoning an unfamiliar word here and there, was all too clear.

> 'The following letter has been received by the editor, dropped into the office letter-box presumably during the hours of darkness. As a matter of extreme public interest we publish it entire. We do not express any opinion on its contents, apart from having satisfied ourselves that the older Gelder certainly was arrested and executed in the circumstances here described, and that the letter contains personal matter of such a nature that we accept its authorship as that of the dead man's son.'

The letter followed.

> 'The town of Gries-am-See is being asked to celebrate the return of a distinguished son in Lucas Corinth, who is held up not only as a fine composer, which he may well be, but also as a hero of the wartime resistance, a title to which

his claim is spurious. It is true that he worked, as a young man, with my father in keeping open an escape route into Switzerland for anti-Nazis threatened with imprisonment and death. It is not true that he is therefore a hero. He was not tested until his own safety was at stake, and that test he failed.'

The story followed in scrupulous detail, except that it was seen from another pole. And there was one important omission. No mention was made of Helmut Vogel, waiting in hiding in the hay-hut on the alm. Valentine Gelder had, of necessity, told his wife about the arrangements for his own departure, and therefore had also told her about the planned meeting with Lucas at the Filsertal gate. He had not told her, and therefore she had not told her son, anything about the affairs of other men, but only what she needed and had a right to know. For what is not confided cannot be extracted, and ignorance would be a partial protection for her. No, there were only two characters in this drama, the man and the boy who made an appointment to meet at the gate at eleven o'clock. The man who went there faithfully, because of the boy, though he already knew the time was running out, and waited, and waited. And the boy who got back into Gries to find the opening of the Filsertal cordoned off, and who was never seen or heard of again in the town, by a single soul, until news came through that he was safely in Switzerland. The boy who did not attempt to come to the meeting place, but took to his heels thankfully, skirting the foothills where there was no patrol, and never stopped running until he was over the border.

'Lucas Corinth abandoned my father to save himself, and has enjoyed, unquestioned, his role of hero while my father suffered torture and death. In the interests of truth I make known the real facts concerning him. In the interests of justice I accept it as my role to redress the balance, and require the price of my father's life from the man who might have saved it, and instead took advantage of circumstances to make sure of saving his own.'

It was signed, and the signature was reproduced, though the letter was typed. 'Valentine Gelder'. Type can be good evidence of origin, but not unless you find the typewriter itself, and how many are there in Gries? Handwriting can be identified, but not unless a specimen of the actual hand turns up for comparison. And for any such investigation, the great need is time, Una thought, and time is just what we haven't got.

'Yes,' said Lucas, slowly and clearly. 'Yes, I see. Indeed I do see how grave a matter it is for the festival, and for you.' The slight note of satire in his careful omission of himself didn't prevent his voice from being the bleakest and saddest sound Una had ever heard.

'Grave? It is monstrous! It could cause a complete boycott. We must take action this very day, you must see that for yourself. Any delay could be fatal, with so much at stake. My reputation . . . all the time and money I have ploughed into this festival . . . You understand what this could do to my prospects?'

My prospects! Lucas had merely anticipated by a few seconds, his intuition was always acute. The truth was coming out now with a vengeance. Graf had a lot to gain by a successful season, in prestige, in local influence, above all in money, with future events in view, and those superhotels just taking shape. He'd brought home the strayed lion, and rubbed his hands over a great coup; but if it was turning out a mangy sort of lion, after all, he wouldn't be particular how he rid himself of it, provided he himself got out clean.

'It isn't true, of course?' he shot out bluntly, with a belligerence which meant that it had better not be true.

'I tend to avoid "of course" in commenting on human actions. But as you say, it isn't true.'

'Then we must take steps instantly to brand this Gelder as the liar he is.'

'That hardly follows,' said Lucas, lifting his pale face sharply. 'What he alleges against me is not true. I didn't leave his father to die. I did come to the meeting-place as soon as I could, and I didn't leave until I knew that he'd been taken, and I couldn't hope to save him. This boy is mistaken. But he is not therefore a liar. Clearly he believes what he says.'

'Mr Corinth, I'm not interested in his motives. As far as I'm concerned one who spreads lies is a liar, and I'll call him what he is. If you didn't run off with the papers at the first sign of danger, and leave him there waiting for you – and of course, you didn't?'

He stared hard into the drawn face that confronted him, still more than half afraid that his enterprise and initiative had only landed him with an indefensible liability. Great composer or not, if Lucas turned out to be a handicap rather than an asset to this man's personal plans, if he could not be publicly and gloriously cleared of this charge against him, then he would be ditched as ostentatiously and brutally as possible, to absolve Graf from any suspicion of loyalty to his bad bargain. It was all shamelessly clear. Valentine Gelder had hit Lucas as hard as he could; but that was a clean blow, it seemed to Una, compared with the tactics of which Herr Graf would be capable. Even his attitude now seemed a worse insult than the accusations of cowardice and treachery.

'I did not,' said Lucas quietly.

'Then it's a simple matter to reply to this. And you must. In justice to me, you must, Mr Corinth. He's given his account of the way you left Gries, you must give yours. Equally publicly.'

'Certainly, whenever you please.'

'If Mr Corinth would care to dictate,' said Crista, from the corner to which she had withdrawn when this confrontation began, 'I will gladly take down his statement and type it for him.'

Una gave her a flashing look of gratitude and liking for the unchanged deference with which she had spoken Lu's name. But Graf shook his head decidedly.

'No, that's not good enough. Let this boy nobody's ever heard of purvey his calumnies in letters to the editor. For us to do that would be undignified. No, a press conference is what we want. Today! Without reference to this business. We know that's what they'll want to ask about, but we don't have to introduce the subject. There are correspondents here just now serving national and even international papers. All that is at our disposal, why shouldn't we use it? You're our visiting celebrity, it's natural I should call a conference for you. Well, what do you say?'

Lucas said: 'I'm prepared to face a press conference whenever you choose to call it. Can you get them together today?'

'After that?' The gesturing hand almost swept the paper to the floor. 'They'd come running in five minutes.'

He was beginning to take heart again, to see the advantages there could be in this sensation; provided, of course, that Corinth had a complete and irrefutable answer to the charges. And he'd better have!

'Three o'clock this afternoon, in the conference room here. Leave the press to me, I'll have them here. Will that do for you?'

'Perfectly,' said Lucas. He said it well, but Una, watching every quiver of his face across the room, knew that he would almost rather have died.

CHAPTER FIVE

With the departure of Herr Graf some kind of atmospheric oppression seemed to have been lifted from the room. All three of the people left behind there in the sudden, blessed, sunlit silence stood mute and motionless for a full minute, coming gradually back to the realisation of mild outward things like the pattern of the damask on the walls, and the thin curl of blue smoke that still crept up out of the ash-tray from Lu's last cigarette before the lightning struck. They stirred and looked at one another. Crista, the first to move, went silently and picked up the fallen sheets of the *Zeitung*, and crumpled them away into the waste-paper basket. Not with any passion or emotion, simply as one disposing of what was finished with, and clearing the ground for whatever was to happen next.

'So it's out in the open,' said Una, and was almost startled by the resolute ring of her own voice. 'Now we know.'

'Now everyone knows,' said Lucas, and with hands at this pass admirably steady lit another cigarette. 'I find it preferable this way.' He didn't say he found it less than excruciating, all the same. He tended to use words with a rather extreme degree of precision, and resented their misuse by others.

'Lu, I'm coming with you to this press conference.'

'No,' he said, 'you are not.'

'Think what you're doing! He isn't calling it to refute anything. Ostensibly, anyhow,' she said impatiently, seeing him open his mouth to argue the point.

'You *are* here as a celebrity. As *the* celebrity. Yesterday was the opening day. Today he calls the press to talk with his star performer. And that's what you have to be, until the bombs start falling. And I am known to be here with you, your darling daughter, and what's more natural than that I should be present at your press conference? Or more unnatural than that I should be absent? I am ammunition, father dear, and you're wasting your assets if you don't fire me.'

'I never liked fire-arms,' said Lucas, almost absently. 'I was never any good with them, either.'

'I'm rather special ammunition. More of a self-guided missile, really.'

'I believe you! But no, love! *Don't*!' he said on a sharp note of displeasure and pain, seeing her brace herself to override him. 'If you were there it would be harder for me.'

He turned his back on her, not abruptly but with aching self-restraint, walked gently into his own room, and closed the door. She looked round at Crista, who stood retired into distance and anonymity, with hooded eyes and oblivious face, rendering herself absent even while she was unable to withdraw and let them alone. Una declined to be ignored, even thus considerately. She was not good at pretending, and saw no future in it now.

'What do you do?' she inquired helplessly. 'What do you say in answer to that?'

Crista was not happy. This must have been a shattering day for her. Una had not forgotten the responsive quivering of that correct little oval face while Lu's hand lay close to hers on the table here, or her loyal offer to record his testimony in his own defence.

'Fathers can be hell,' Una admitted wryly, 'especially when they're widowers.' And personable, she thought, but did not say.

'It could be true,' said Crista earnestly, 'what he says. That you would make it harder for him.'

'It is true, I know that. It could also be true that I should be useful to him. His life doesn't consist just of this afternoon, and he owes me something too.' She meant it. Who was he to shield his too-thin spiritual skin with a body and presence that meant so much to at least one other living being? Sometimes she could have clouted him, and rejoiced in his astonished and daunted revaluation of her in consequence.

'If it is of any help,' said Crista, 'I will come and stay with you this afternoon, while he goes to this conference.'

It occurred to Una then that it was sensitive of her not to offer to arrange a trip to the circus, or something, to distract the anxious daughter while the press crucified the father. Perhaps she really did feel some of the currents that raged about her. And perhaps she had a genuine glimpse of what Lu would be experiencing when he faced his dissectors.

'That's very kind of you,' she said. 'I'd like you to.'

'I think *he* would like me to,' said Crista.

It was five o'clock before they came up from the conference room, Lucas, Herr Graf, and the elderly stranger with the mild, weather-beaten face.

Crista had come to spend the waiting time with Una, as she had promised, had ordered tea for her, filled up the dragging moments as well as she could, and blessedly refrained from being either cheerful and rallying or hushed and over-sympathetic. They had been only too well apprised of the influx of newsmen by the sound of car after car turning in on the fine gravel of the forecourt. By mutual consent they said not a word of Lucas.

The tea had been removed long before they heard voices in the corridor, and a hand at the outer door.

'They are here,' said Crista, rising, and reached at once for her handbag. 'I will have fresh tea sent up as I go, shall I?'

Then the first emphatic voice erupted into the room

ahead of its owner, and the first voice, naturally, belonged to Heinz-Otto Graf, in mid-sentence and stopping for no man.

'—very well, we have now to plan our own strategy. This is to be a council of war. What we have just done is only the first move. Defence is not enough, we have to attack. Let us sit down and consider how to spike this maniac's guns.'

His metaphors, Una thought with dislike, but also with a degree of sour and reluctant amusement, were not only juvenile but absurdly out of date. But his energy was real enough, and his ruthlessness was beyond question. He looked round the room with the eye of a proprietor – it was, after all, his hotel! – observed Crista unobtrusively preparing to leave as soon as the others had entered, omitted her from the perfunctory grunt of greeting he directed at Una – Crista, after all, was his employee, practically his property! – and issued instead an order and a dismissal: 'We shan't require your services now, Fräulein Lohr, but I shall have occasion to get in touch with you later this evening. You'll be at home, if I call you in, say, an hour?'

'Fräulein Lohr is very welcome to stay, if she would like to,' said Lucas, giving her a brief and shadowed smile. 'I have every confidence in her.'

'Thank you,' she said gravely. 'But I have things I must do, if you'll excuse me.' And to Graf: 'I will be in my flat, if you wish to telephone me.'

The stranger held the door for her, and closed it gently after her when she was gone. He came forward into the room, a big, rangy, lean man of about sixty, with a mountaineer's long bones and wind-burned skin, and blue, bright, far-sighted eyes. Short curls of crisp iron-grey hair clustered at his temples and fringed a bald scalp, polished and tanned to glossy Indian red.

'This is Herr Dieter Wehrle,' said Lucas. 'My daughter.' A seamed brown hand, a countryman's hand, engulfed Una's fingers. 'Herr Wehrle is chief of police here in Gries.'

'He did not call me in,' said Wehrle, observing the questioning glance Una darted at her father. He had the mountain man's vast, deep but quiet voice, a murmur out of a cavern, and a smile that creased the corners of his eyes. 'I can also read.'

'I'm glad you're here,' said Una truthfully; all the more because it seemed clear that he had not been summoned to the press conference by Herr Graf, either, and almost certainly he was not in that indefatigable collector's possession. 'I wanted to come to you from the beginning.'

Lucas crossed to the table and helped himself to a cigarette. He looked drawn and tired, and the faint, fastidious disgust that showed in his eyes and lips told her all too clearly how he had been handled. She watched him narrowly, and asked, with some hesitancy: 'How did it go? They weren't – hostile?'

Faint surprise lightened the load of his wretchedness at that. What on earth had the friendliness or hostility of the press to do with the lacerations its embrace left on his flesh? It was almost worse to be caressed than to be clawed.

'Hostile? No more hostile than a Rugby scrum is to the ball. They're not for or against, just hungry for a row, and they think they're on to one. Oh, no, it went all right, I suppose. I answered everything they asked me, I can't do any more.'

'You could have been a little less deprecating,' said Graf with displeasure, grinding out his long cheroot in the ashtray with unnecessary violence. 'I'm doing my best for you, Mr Corinth, in very difficult circumstances. I understand that you're unwilling to parade your achievements. But you must realise that Gries has been looking upon you as a hero of the underground movement during the war, not simply as a gifted composer. There was no need to refuse laurels quite so ungraciously.'

Una closed her eyes for a second in mute resignation. She could see it all, the avid correspondents peppering him with questions, some provocative, some sympathetic, some probably malevolent, Graf offering him lead after lead, prompting him to an appropriately large performance, and Lucas stubbornly refusing every opening, with that expression of incredulous distaste on his face, and those deliberate, curt understatements in his mouth. If they hadn't been hostile at the beginning, ten to one they were at the end. The press doesn't like having its standards publicly disdained. Who does?

Once, long ago, in the days of her first motherly devotion, she remembered packing him off to clinch his application for the post of conductor to some provincial orchestra, and threatening to send him there with a label round his neck: Caution! Does not interview well! And when he had failed to ingratiate himself and come back without the job she had scolded him bitterly for an arrogance calculated to put up even the most insensitive provincial back. That was at eleven years old; now that she was turned twenty she was resigned to taking him as he was, and making the best of it.

'If you've represented me as any sort of hero,' said Lucas, colouring hotly, 'you've done so without my knowledge or consent, and I can't be responsible for the results. I've told my side of the story, and I've no reason to believe that it won't be fairly reported. But I won't lay myself out to court favour by pretending to be what I'm not.'

'More important now,' said Wehrle, in the voice of unmistakable and undisputed authority, 'is to make all possible dispositions for your safety, Mr Corinth.' He flashed one glance of his sharp eyes at Una. 'I am not sure if Miss Corinth knows the exact position . . . ?'

'She knows.'

'Including the threats to your life?'

'If we are to look upon them as that, yes. Please do sit down. I'm neglecting my duty. Will you drink something? Whisky? Or would you prefer tea?'

'Whisky will be ideal.' Wehrle sat back in the offered chair, and spread his large hands on his knees. 'I think we are to look upon them as precisely that. Threats are made, even in bizarre circumstances, without any serious intent or ability to carry them out. We know it happens. I see no symptoms here of the kind of histrionic or hysteric personality that looks for fulfilment in that way. The letter, you must have observed, is remarkably lucid, literate and precise. The intent rings only too true. And I think even the ability may not be lacking. But even if I did not see so much in the threat itself to impress me, I could not possibly assume that it was not to be taken seriously.'

'I suppose not,' Lucas agreed dubiously.

'The first consideration, therefore, is to take good care of you, and make a criminal approach, as nearly as we can, impossible. The second is to try and trace Frau Gelder's movements after she left Gries, and find out what happened to her son, and run him to earth if we can. But it's going to take us some days, at least. I have already set things in motion on the obvious lines open to us, beginning in Linz, where she came from.'

'Nobody knows what the boy looks like?' Lucas asked.

'As far as we know he has never been in Gries, or at least never under his own name. No one has seen him, no one knows what he looks like. All we know is that he would now be around twenty-seven years old. He may be here in the town at this moment, calling himself Schmidt or Müller. The only other lead we have to him is this letter to the *Zeitung*. Naturally that is being carefully examined, and any leads we can get out of it will be followed up. Then there is also the matter of providing all possible confirmation of your story. If he could be convinced, he might – surely he would if he is not mad – abandon his purpose. It is perfectly understandable that you avoided encountering anyone who might know you, that evening you came back from Innsbruck, but it leaves us few opportunities. There was the other man you took over the border with you. Yes, yes, I know you told me he was old, and is dead many years ago, but nevertheless there must be records of your arrival with him in Switzerland, where everything is so orderly – even of his movements afterwards. Every grain of corroboration is valuable. I am contacting the Swiss authorities about him. Did he stay there, or did he also go to England?'

'He died in Zurich,' said Lucas. 'I hadn't been in touch with him for years, I heard about it only when I received a notice of his funeral. They must have found my name and address among his papers. There was a widow – he'd married again in his old age.'

'Then there are threads to be found, and we shall find them.'

Late, and at second hand, thought Una practically. An old woman, widowed fourteen years ago, asked to remember something her husband may have mentioned another fourteen years before that. No, why give a thought to that faint and feeble possibility?

'Then there is the man to whom you spoke in the woods, and to whom you committed the legitimation that was meant for Gelder. And the colleague to whom this stranger was to deliver it.'

'That will hardly get us far,' said Lucas wearily. 'Bruchmann is also dead. Nor can he ever have received the message. We'd already thought of that line of inquiry. Fräulein Lohr rang the saw-mill and asked about him this morning. He was arrested in that same drive. He died in a concentration camp.'

'Which leaves only the stranger. Oh, I know you've already told this incident in detail – or you think you have. But I need every grain of evidence I can get about him, if I'm to look for him with any hope of finding him. And there are certain limited guides already. Not a native, you thought. More than that, not a settled man – all the indications were of a travelling man. The regulars come year after year to the fair. I shall have men on the fairground all day tomorrow, and I myself shall be there tonight. We have a limitation of age – a man, if not exactly as you estimated, nevertheless considerably older than yourself. We need not look at anyone below fifty-five. Also some indication of stature. You say he was taller than you, and you are by no means a short man, though perhaps then you had not quite all your growth. In the dark there is no colouring, I know. He could stand abnormally still when needful. And he had a sack with him.'

'I took him to be a poacher,' said Lucas simply.

'Which also goes with the fairground,' agreed Wehrle drily. 'Tell me again what he told you. No, don't elaborate, the same words will do – the words you used instinctively may even be very significant.'

'He said he had heard a man grappled with and overpowered, heard him challenged by the name of Valentine Gelder, and heard him admit to his identity. He didn't recognise the voice, and didn't know the name. He simply reported what he heard.'

'Anything else you recall? However trivial?'

'He never looked directly at me. In the dark one strains to see. He stood all the time with his head turned sideways to me. But that didn't surprise me. The times were like that. He didn't want to show his face too clearly to anyone, even another fugitive. Even in the dark.'

'Yet you did trust each other. You gave him the message to carry. And he accepted it and promised to deliver it.'

'Yes. It wasn't his fault that he couldn't do it.'

'Nothing more?'

Lucas shook his head. 'I can think of nothing.'

'Very well, we must make the best of what we

have.' He had made no notes on paper, but he had been storing away details methodically in that weather-beaten skull of his. 'And now to make the best arrangements we can for your protection meantime. Herr Graf has made a suggestion which may serve very well.'

'I am responsible for your safety,' said Graf heavily, 'since I brought you here.' His tone said that he was still pondering whether to repent the move or no; for after all, if public opinion veered in Lucas's direction the whole affair might yet record a credit balance. 'We're all agreed that the festival must go on according to plan. There's too much at stake to cancel it now. There's only one course open to us, to go ahead as though nothing had happened, as though it's taken for granted that the public will accept our side of the story. But you must cooperate in the additional precautions we're forced to take for your protection against this crazy young man. I suggest that you and Miss Una shall move from this hotel at once – of course without giving up these rooms and without any publicity – and take up residence on my island. It need not inconvenience you at all. I have a boat which shall be always at your disposal. One wing of the hotel is already hab-itable, there is power, and the telephone, and I am arranging that the kitchen there shall be provisioned with everything you will need for a short stay. The con-version work has ceased for the time being, because of the festival, there is no one resident there. I would give you a housekeeper, but the fewer people who know where you are, the better. If Miss Una will be able to manage the household . . . ?'

Una looked out at the green and white pyramid of rocks and rose-coloured roofs across the water of the lake, the long finger of rock and jetty that pointed towards it from the foundations of the castle, and the blue moat that surrounded it.

'I can manage, I'm sure. It sounds to me a very good idea.'

'I will send Fräulein Lohr over there with you, since

she already knows so much about this affair, and she can get in touch immediately with me or with Herr Wehrle here. She accepted the special assignment to act as your personal secretary during your visit, as all my office knows, it will look better if she continues in the same capacity. I shall be much happier when I know you have the Himmelsee all round you. An attacker would have to swim or take a boat to reach you, he could hardly do so without being seen. I should like you to make the move this evening,' he said briskly. 'Please be ready in about one hour, and I will have the boat pick you up then.'

The tone was enough to raise Lucas's hackles and make him refuse to move, but he was too deeply aware of the trouble he was already causing, however involuntarily, to wish to add to it, and he could feel Una's eagerness and relief. He agreed stiffly: 'Very well! Naturally I want to do what I can to help.'

'You could have done that rather more effectively,' said Wehrle, good-humouredly enough, 'if you'd reported those telephone calls to me as soon as you received them. There might have been a chance of tracing them if we'd known in time. I doubt if there'll be any more from now on. But I propose to send two of my young men over to the island with you, if you'll humour me. They'll be in plain clothes, and I've no doubt they'll find the assignment as good as a holiday. But they'll also be armed. And efficient. You'll oblige me by co-operating with them, even if you don't enjoy the experience of having a bodyguard. I'm merely doing my job. For the moment, Mr Corinth, you *are* my job.'

'The boat will be below at the hotel stage in one hour,' said Graf, rising. 'You can leave part of your luggage here, I will see that it's safe.'

They were already withdrawing when he turned in the doorway to say, almost apologetically, as if in conciliation for all his minor offences: 'You will like the villa. It's a beautiful property – it used to be the summer residence belonging to the castle. But of course, you're a native, you must remember it well. Did you know it used to be known as the Himmelhof?'

'Charming!' said Lucas, the faint glitter of a real smile kindling in his eyes. 'But not, I hope, to be taken as an omen!'

CHAPTER SIX

It was Jörg-Erich who came for them at the end of their hour of grace, tapping discreetly at the door of their suite, with one of Dieter Wehrle's young men at his heels.

'The boat is down at the stage, and Fräulein Lohr is there already, with Herr Geestler's colleague. May I present Hugo Geestler? Mr Corinth – Miss Una. We can go down from the balcony to the terraces, and so to the jetty. It will be more unobtrusive. Though of course, to take a boat out across the lake in the early evening is most usual – not at all for comment. Let me take your bag, Miss Una. Believe me, we shall do everything to take the best care of you.'

He was as handsome, as smooth, as sunny as ever, his deference towards Lucas and his patent admiration for Una had not changed in the slightest degree. He was, Una thought, the silky side of Graf's rough and forceful proprietorship, and groomed for that very purpose; but exactly how much of him was real she could no longer estimate. He acted rather like an heir apparent. Yet she doubted if Graf himself knew half of what went on inside that beautifully barbered blond head. Or anyone else, for that matter, except Jörg-Erich Fischer. But she was grateful for his surface kindness.

Hugo Geestler was a stocky young man, thick set and powerful, like most of the locals, but quick and neat of movement, with the massively boned face and loose, easy bearing of mountain-dwellers everywhere. If he had luggage for his stay, he had already stowed it in the boat, for he was dressed in good grey slacks and a short-sleeved sports-shirt, like any nice girl's boating escort on a summer evening, and hid his wide-set brown eyes, when they emerged into sunlight, behind the trendy square-rimmed dark glasses of the season. He hoisted Lucas's modest bag under one arm, turning it into the mere repository for an evening picnic, or something equally transient. He smiled, but so far he had said nothing beyond a shy murmur of greeting in the universal bass-baritone of the valley, cavernous even when venting a sigh.

'Do you speak English?' Una asked him on the steps leading down to the terrace. She hardly knew why, for her German was coming to life now, and emergency had given her the vigour to pursue it without tiring. Perhaps she needed to know how much this young man was going to understand of what she might have to say to Lu in their withdrawn moments. For after all, Valentine Gelder the Younger was – must be – twenty-seven years old, and how many months on either side of twenty-seven could Hugo Geestler be?

'A little,' he said modestly. 'Richard knows it better. But I understand.'

'And you know all about us? About what's happened?'

'I know,' said the deep voice.

Lucas was in front with Jörg-Erich; she had this unknown young man with the screened eyes to herself for these few moments, and felt an urgent need to probe deeper than his skin. She looked sidelong at him as they descended the steps, and saw a profile like the severe weathering of rock, very clean and hard and pure. The trouble was that she could envisage Valentine Gelder in just such an image, aloof and unassailable within his delusion, adamant in his judgement, proof against all appeal in his rocky certainty.

'And you like this assignment?'

She had forgotten, or some intuitive sensitivity had told her to forget, and she spoke this time in German, a shock question that somehow did not shock.

'I like,' said Hugo Geestler, still and imperviously in English, though he had to filter his words in that strange language one by one through his deliberate mind, 'music.' It was a declaration of faith. 'I play – not well – piano, organ, any keyboard. Yes, I like.'

She had her answer. And here they were on the white flags of the hotel jetty, the slanting evening light sending up splinters of radiance from the quivering wavelets into their eyes. The Himmelsee was a very placid lake, sheltered and immune. The wind played with it; never assaulted it. The aloof Silvretta saw to that. The motorboat that rode silkily under the steps did no more than finger the stone frontage with its round nylon fenders. Crista was in it, and the second young man.

'Richard Schwalbe,' introduced Jörg-Erich amiably, handing down first Una, and then Lucas, into the boat.

'Charmed!' said Richard Schwalbe, with something of a flourish, gripping Una's hand firmly and warmly. And he wore no sun-glasses, and his eyes were black and bright and happily appreciative, not missing the movement of her long, agile legs as she dropped aboard, or a curve of her body as she moved to a seat beside Crista in the stern. He was an inch or two taller than Geestler, but a good many pounds lighter, a long, athletic youngster with a lively face ready to laugh, and a bush of curling dark hair. He received the bags airily, one-handed, and stowed them with economic movements, rather like calculated moves in a game. He was in shorts and a bright tee-shirt. Una had never seen anyone who looked less like a police officer.

Jörg-Erich hovered, attentive to the last, as they seated themselves and turned their eyes expectantly towards the lofty islet over half a mile away.

'I have been out there and checked that there are plenty of provisions and bedding, everything you will need. Oh, yes, and you'll find the letters from the afternoon post in the drawing-room, Mr Corinth. I collected them from the festival office and took them straight over with me, as I was going across.'

'You've been very kind,' Lucas said.

'Not at all! If there is anything you need, anything I've forgotten, please call me, don't hesitate. I will come out at any time.'

Schwalbe started the engine, and shoved off lightly from the landing-stage, and the boat turned and drew away steadily towards the island. As they neared it they lost sight of the coronal of rose-red roof tiles, white walls and foaming green trees, and were left facing, on this townward side, a sheer face of pleated and striated cliff with a reef of rocks at its foot. A short, narrow spur jutted out from the centre, and a small view-tower crowned it, arching rococo brows to stare across at the castle.

'The lantern,' said Crista, pointing. 'It is joined by a narrow corridor to the back of the Himmelhof. Like a look-out tower.'

'But how do we get up there?' asked Una, eyeing the almost vertical rocks that reared out of the placid water.

'The jetty is at the other side. You will see, the whole island is like a tiered stage, sloping down to the south-west. We have to round this southern point, then there's a small beach, and beyond it the landing-stage. Everything here faces the same way, the house turns its back on the town. When you see the view from the terrace you will see why. Every morning to wake up and see that view! No people, no buildings but your own house, just the lake and the far shore, and up above, the Silvretta. Such peace!' she said, for once with a note of urgency and passion in her voice that made Una turn and look at her in mild surprise.

'They orientated the house towards the sun, of course,' she said. 'The beach faces due south, there's good, safe bathing there.'

Schwalbe brought the boat round well clear of the southern point, and they came into a little bay where the water shaded off from deepest blue through paling shades of green as the yellow sand showed through. Beyond the scalloped rim of beach a long arm of low rocks curved out again into the water, and terminated in a short stone jetty. Here the sheer rocks drew back to reveal an improbable baroque stage-set, ornate staircases climbing from the sands, terrace after railed terrace, pavilion beyond pavilion, half overgrown with untended shrubs and flowering trees, and studded with massive stone vases and marble nymphs and satyrs, to a glimpse of the white house on the crest.

'There is another jetty on the northern side,' Crista said, 'you can cross from there very quickly to the castle. A path leads down to it from the northern end of the terrace. But this will be the main entrance for the hotel, when it is finished. Because of the beach, of course, that will be one of the main assets. And I think Herr Graf is also planning a swimming-pool on top, close to the house. But the work is only begun. The interior has never been totally neglected, but of course no one has been resident except a caretaker, it is dilapidated in places. Please take care on the stair-cases, they are very chipped and broken here and there, and of course bringing up building materials hasn't helped. But there's no point in repairing them until everything is finished.'

The boat, its engine mute, slid neatly along the stage, and Geestler leaned out from the bow, and made it fast. They climbed ashore and began to mount the first stairway. At each level the path changed its direction, and sometimes its nature, a slope of gravel replacing the steps. Gradually the house on its final great terrace rose into view, a central rectangular block with a classic portico, its cornice ornamented with six carved nymphs; and two lower wings, curving round, one on either side, to make a semicircle open to the south-west. Over the ornate stone railings and balustrades great sheaves of green and cascades of flowers hung. Crista had been right about the broken state of the steps, there were stones displaced and cracked here and there, retaining walls had shed great flakes of plaster, and were patterned with enigmatic maps of imaginary lands. The ceramic vases that fringed the paths were grey with lichens. As they approached the house itself they could see that its plaster was peeling, too, shutters dangled by one hinge at some windows, festoons of stucco garlands had shed half their flowers, tubs were falling apart and spilling soil from their overgrown decorative trees. Clearly Herr Graf had only recently decided to restore the place to its original grandeur, the process had not yet gone very far. But it had a mellowed, decrepit baroque beauty just as it was. It was probably more attractive now in its desolation, Una thought, than it had ever been in its heyday, or would ever be again.

'To the right,' directed Crista as they reached the semicircular forecourt. 'This southern wing is where we shall be living. This has been – not yet restored, but at least made habitable.'

The two wings were only one storey high, but a lofty storey, and a narrow, covered colonnade, supported on slender pillars, lined the curve. The rooms made ready for them were at the end of the wing. There was a great salon, the final room of all, that went right through the wing, and had windows both on the lake and the terrace, an array of smaller bedrooms opening from an inner corridor and looking out over the water, a bathroom, a kitchen, and well-stocked store cupboards. They would be sleeping under gold and white ceilings panelled with allegorical paintings at once elegant and tawdry, and viewing themselves in mirrors airborne by pneumatic amoretti. The furniture, as yet, was still the original, rococo satins and gilt, pastel brocades falling, here and there, into threadbare lace, and even into holes. But to judge by the newly-fitted kitchen and plumbing, this suite would one day be the private apartment of Herr Graf's manager, when the new luxury hotel was opened at last.

The cabinets in the salon still held fine glass, china figures that looked like Meissen, ivory fans, snuff-boxes, all their treasures. The chairs and slender-legged sofas were of white and gilt, upholstered in palest blue brocade. It was easy to see that this had been an appanage of the castle; it had all the excesses, and still retained the shameless charm. Una was so fascinated by it that for the first hour she almost forgot the reason for their exile here.

The bustle of installing themselves and examining their palatial prison kept them occupied for some time. Geestler and Schwalbe had brought up more cartons of provisions from the boat, including a case of whisky, Lucas noted with some amusement. *By way of anaesthesia, or am I thought to be so anglicised that I cannot exist without it? Gin, too! The essentials were all taken care of.* There were beds for everyone, and these young men of Wehrle's seemed to be expecting to cater for themselves, and spend their time, watch and watch about, outside Lucas's door. Una would probably have something to say about the catering, with a new electric cooker at her disposal, and all those stores in the kitchen cupboards. She would be planning to feed everyone.

She was; and Dieter Wehrle's young men accepted her summons to dinner with the greatest complacency. It was a summer meal of cold meats, cheeses, pickles and salads, in view of the hour, but she had produced, by way of masterpiece, a sweet omelette of heroic proportions, whipped to the table with exact timing which had cost her a considerable expenditure in nervous energy, and repaid her with copious compliments. Briefly and miraculously, in the middle of the hurricane, where the core of calm rests, Una was utterly happy. Lucas was devoutly grateful for that, even if it lasted no more than a breath. He had written and posted his letter to his solicitor; he was ready, he had his own measure of repose.

The two girls were washing up in the kitchen, after all the coffee had been drunk and all the hopeful spurt of conversation had subsided into those separate silences to which Lucas was so accustomed, where everyone walked alone. The two young men had withdrawn to patrol their domain and examine all its defences, to pinpoint the stations that controlled the best views over the Himmelsee, and check all the approaches before the darkness came down on them.

In a sense Lucas had been waiting for this moment when he would be alone in the salon. Alone, you come to grips with the reality about yourself, the things that matter most to you, and those that are dispensable. In the salon, its table now cleared of the communal feast, there was, not a piano – such modernities would have been out of place here – but a very beautiful harpsichord, so polished and immaculate that he dared suppose someone had been tending it during the years of its silence. No wire strings, either! The old, dulcet tone, distant and plaintive. There might be mute keys, he had to be prepared for that. It would be preferable to a modern mock-up in mint order.

He had kept his hands from it until now. He caressed the exquisite, glossy wood, so harmoniously grained, like a perfect, tideless sea. And his eyes lit, inescapably, upon the neat little pile of letters arrayed upon its cover, accurately in the middle, to ensure that they should not be overlooked. Of course! Jörg-Erich had brought over with him the mail received at the festival office. Lucas had had all his letters directed there, in ignorance of the arrangements made for his accommodation.

There was no escaping the world. Resignedly he picked up and shuffled the meagre pile. Not so many people had found it imperative to remember the existence of Lucas Corinth; a salutary reflection. Three letters from friends in England – perhaps it was not so bad a score to record three genuine friends! – one from his agent, no doubt about some autumn booking, a card from his dead wife's sister on holiday in Brittany – she had never approved of her sister's marriage! – and one unstamped envelope, apparently unmailed, addressed to him via the festival office in characterless block letters.

He stood looking at the mute, anonymous thing in his hand, searching the blue-black ball-pen lines of the superscription, bracing himself to open it. There was nothing in it but a slip of manuscript paper, with a few bars of music scribbled on it. He stared at the scrawled notes for a long moment, then he opened the harpsichord, very gently and reverently, and fingered them out on the keys. It wasn't necessary; he knew already what they were, and what they meant, and they needed no signature.

He had accepted the need to cooperate now, he was the centre of an elaborate and expensive police operation, and he had no choice but to confide everything, even this, which by its very expression seemed to him almost too intimate a communication to be shared with any other creature. Regretfully he went out into the colonnade, where the windows of the wing opposite flashed the reflection of the setting sun into his eyes. Such large windows, like those of the salon here, that he could clearly see the shrouded shapes of delicate furniture within, and the bright, opalescent eye of a rounded mirror on the wall. Hugo Geestler was coming back up the steps from his circuit of the house and terraces.

'Herr Geestler, will you come in for a moment? There has been . . .' He wasn't sure what to call it. 'A development.'

'You've seen someone? An intruder?' The young man came springing up the last staircase three at a time.

'No, no, nothing has happened. Simply another message. If I'm not reading too much into it.' But he knew he was not. It was a fitting, even a chivalrous touch, to send him his warnings in music. 'You remember Herr Fischer said he had brought the mail over with our provisions? I have only just got round to opening it. This envelope – perhaps we ought not to handle it? Though of course I already have!'

Geestler crossed the room with him, and bent his head to examine the envelope where it lay, without touching. The two girls were just coming from the kitchen, and Una came curiously to see what was being inspected so carefully. The distractions and charms of the Himmelhof had so effectively restored her innocence that at first she had no thought of any- thing sinister, and said eagerly, remembering this young man's professed interest in keyboard music: 'Yes, why don't we have a concert? I bet the acoustics in here would be ideal for a harpsichord.'

Then she saw the torn scrap of paper on which all their attention had been focused, and instantly the shadow came down again upon her face.

'What is it?' She looked from the spray of black notes scored deeply into the paper, to Lucas's face.

'It is exactly what you see. It was here among the letters – now that I think back, in the middle of the sheaf.'

'It has not been through the post,' said Geestler. 'This has something to do with Gelder? For I think you know what it means.'

'Yes, I know what it means. You don't recognise it?' He picked out the notes again on the keyboard, and sang the first bar or two in a soft, thoughtful voice: ' *"Heut' oder Morgen . . ."* It's the Marschallin in "Rosenkavalier", at the end of the last act, remembering what she herself said in the first.

"Today or tomorrow; if not tomorrow, very soon."
But he hasn't carried the quotation to the end of the
phrase, so I take it to mean just what it says. Today –
not much left of today, now, but still a few hours – or
tomorrow. I'm being given fair warning, and time to
say my prayers.'

'*Lu!*' cried Una on a muted gasp of protest, and
plucked his hand from the keys as though she had
caught him in the act of opening a door to his own
murderer.

Geestler, without a word, picked up the telephone
and dialled. In the few minutes of waiting they heard
the light steps of Richard Schwalbe walk the length of
one of the lower terraces, and heard him whistling to
himself: '*Schenkt man sich Rosen in Tirol . . .*'

There would be no one in the festival office at this
hour of the evening. Geestler went straight to Jörg-
Erich's home number, and talked for some minutes in
German too rapid and colloquial for Una to follow.
Then he depressed the rest with a slam of his brown
palm, and held it there briefly.

'Herr Fischer himself collected the letters from the
office. He is quite positive that there was no unmailed
envelope among them, and he didn't let them out of
his hands – or his briefcase, more accurately – until
he put them here on the harpsichord.'

'He had a boatman with him?' asked Lucas.

'He had, but he is sure his briefcase was never
touched, and never laid down out of his sight. It's
second nature to retain a hold on a briefcase, as on a
handbag.'

'They had things to carry into these rooms. They
might well be in and out, separately, two or three
times. It would not be difficult, or take long, to slip
one extra envelope among the others.'

'It would not, but the boatman who brought him
out was one of Herr Graf's employees from long
since, far too old to be connected with this Gelder.
Herr Fischer has given me the number of the girl who

gave him the letters in the office. If she sorted them from other mail she must know whether there was one delivered by hand among them. Herr Fischer might not notice, if it was in the middle of the bunch.'

Jörg-Erich, Una thought but refrained from saying, would know not only how many letters there were, but the post-marks of each, and probably the date of posting, too. Inside information on everything connected with Herr Graf's business interests was surely part of his essential stock-in-trade. It would be interesting, though, if the girl from the office stated firmly that there *had* been one letter delivered by hand.

But she did not. She confirmed Jörg-Erich's statement without hesitation. Geestler cradled the receiver again and sat back, frowning thoughtfully, before he dialled his chief's own number and made his report.

'It was not among the letters in the office, it was not among them when Herr Fischer put them down here. Unless,' he said firmly, 'we are to think that Herr Fischer is lying, and inserted the envelope himself. Or, just as improbable, that Herr Graf's boatman, for some obscure reason, inserted it without Herr Fischer's knowledge before they left the island. Perhaps someone else asked him to do it – either the simple delivery of a message – but then why place it so unobtrusively, and why say nothing about it? – or a furtive errand well paid, and no questions asked.'

'It couldn't have been inserted here,' said Una positively, 'not since then. There's nobody here but us.'

'True,' said Lucas musingly, closing the harpsichord. 'There's nobody here but us.'

How long, he wondered, had these two young men been in the police force, and how long here in Gries? This man might very well be a native, almost certainly was, there had been a whole family of Geestlers here before the war. But the other, the dark boy, Richard Schwalbe – Richard the Swallow . . . *'Es kehret die dunkle Schwalbe, Aus fernem Land zurück . . .'* 'The

dark swallow comes back from foreign lands . . .'
No, there'd never been any Schwalbes in these parts.
And Jörg-Erich himself, what were his antecedents?
Did his employer know all about his family from two
generations back? He was the right age, so far as one
can judge these days. Had any of them a look of
Valentine?

The truth was that he could recall very strongly all
that he had felt for Valentine Gelder as his friend and
his chief, but he had long since forgotten what he
looked like. The face was there in his mind, but
dimmed and half-erased, like a faded photograph. He
made no effort to restore its features. It is very difficult to evade a really punctilious hate, it will find you
no matter what you do. Better to sit quietly and wait
for it. Otherwise there's no end, no peace for the
pursued or the pursuer; and most faithfully, in his
heart, he wished young Valentine peace.

Geestler concluded his call, and cradled the
telephone.

'I must ask you, sir,' he said, politely but firmly, 'to
stay withindoors tonight. We shall keep watch all
night. Obviously the hours of darkness will be the
most dangerous time, but your bedrooms overlook
the water, and the drop is steep, almost sheer. You
will please keep the door of your room locked, and
the curtains drawn.' He had borrowed something of
Wehrle's authoritative tone, and he emphasised it still
more when he saw the weary smile on Lucas's lips. 'I
am responsible for your life now, Mr Corinth, I insist
you shall help and not hinder me.'

'I have a regard for my life, too,' Lucas assured
him. 'I shall obey orders.'

He crossed to the window that overhung the water,
drew it gently to without latching it, and pulled the
curtains close over it. He stood for a moment with the
folds just parted in his hands, looking across the
Himmelsee to the twinkling lights of Gries. The sky
was fully dark now, a dusky purplish blue like the

petals of clematis flowers; only faint, quivering lines
of reflected light transfixed the water of the lake like
spears, and between them flashed occasional phosphorescent glints, as the rising night wind ruffled the
surface with shudders of disquiet. They were out of
reach of all sounds from the shore; the silence here
was profound.

'What a pity,' he thought, 'if I'm never to hear
"The Horn of Roland" performed after all. What a
pity if this is the final silence.'

He froze then, with the curtains still in his hands.
Desire or reality, he was hearing it now, Roland's
horn, in that brilliant threnody he had written for its
last solo passages. They were all hearing it, clear and
close, no illusion. He might hypnotise himself into an
aural hallucination, but not them. Una had come to
his side, he felt her quivering against him. Crista's
black eyes, enormous and deep, seemed to be listening, too, and her fingers, extended on the air, and
even the strand of hair that had fallen loose over her
forehead. Geestler had crossed almost stealthily to
join them at the window, and was searching the dark
water for a betraying ripple.

Somewhere out there, very close to the island,
someone was performing dazzling high, defiant calls
on a horn, drawing out the long, sustained appeals
like threads of spun brass, smooth as honey, sharp as
gall. The last great solo, splendidly played.

Only no one here should have known it! No one
here could possibly know it, except the horn players
of the town orchestra, and the unknown soloist he
was to meet for the first time at tomorrow's rehearsal.

'What is it?' Geestler was demanding urgently,
shaking him by the arm. 'This is something to do with
you, that I have seen. This music you know, something about it you know. What is it? What does it
mean?'

'It's my music,' said Lucas, with remote pleasure
and pride. 'I wrote it. It's the final horn solo from the

work we're to rehearse tomorrow. No one can be playing it but a member of your orchestra. It can be meant for no one but me. What does it mean? According to my programme it means the death of Roland – according to his, I imagine, it means the death of Lucas Corinth.'

CHAPTER SEVEN

Geestler spun on his heel and plunged out of the room, drawing the door to after him with a slam. They heard a shrill whistle outside on the terrace, a quick, light flurry of running feet, a few words called down into the garden, and an answering shout as Schwalbe vaulted one of the walls below, and ran after his colleague.

'The boat!' cried Una, caught up in the gust of their going, and halfway across the colonnade before she realised she was running. 'They're going down to the jetty. They're going to round him up and bring him in.' She halted just as abruptly, and flattened her hands imperiously against her father's chest. 'No, you don't! You've got your orders. You're to stay in and keep the door locked.'

'And let you go rushing down those broken steps to the jetty in the dark,' he said scornfully. The breath of action had brought him to life again, he no longer wanted to sit and wait for fate to come to him, he wanted to go out and look for it. After all, it was the first opportunity he'd had. 'If that's my man out there with the horn,' he said, 'I want to meet him just as urgently as he wants to meet me. You stay here and keep out of the way.'

He had the bit between his teeth now, and she didn't know how she was going to stop him. But neither could he frown her into staying behind; she had no intention of letting him out of her sight. She was hard on his heels as he plunged into the darkness, halting for a moment on the terrace to accustom his eyes to the change.

'He may have a motor-boat, too,' said Crista, close

behind them, her sandals clicking on the uneven stones.

'No! Don't you remember how silent it was, just before we heard the horn? No, he's in a rowing boat, he can't run from them.'

They came scrambling down the curving steps in the dark, terrace after terrace, to the jetty at the far end of the beach, and stood peering out over the lake surface. The engine of the motor-boat purred busily, somewhere out there at the end of its shining track; the ripples of its wash rustled up the beach in the soft sand. The lengthening trail of phosphorescence swept round in a great coil, like an illuminated question-mark, a dotted line of light heaving and twinkling to the play of the disturbed water.

'They're trying to circle round him and drive him in,' cried Una. She strained her eyes upon the patch of water they were ringing, but could not see another boat moving. The horn was silent; they had not noticed the moment when the thin gold tone of its last cry dissolved into the night.

'There!' said Crista, pointing along the line of the rocks. A faint, darting point of light sparkled and vanished, another, nearer the shore, rhythmically appearing and disappearing. 'See the oars dipping! He's rowing in to the rocks.'

Lucas dropped Una's hand and ran, away from the jetty, along the broken, rocky shelves that gnawed at the water, running to meet the incoming boat. He heard Una stumbling after him, and cried to her to go back, but she still followed grimly, until the smooth sole of her sandal slipped on a mossy, slanting stone, and she came down on grazed hands; and then he came leaping back to pick her up and plant her on her feet again almost angrily, because the sound of her fall had shaken and touched him more than he dared admit.

'Why can't you do as you're told? Here, if you must come, hold on to my arm.'

'Why can't you?' she said heatedly. 'You're supposed to be safe in the house. I'm damned well not letting you out of my sight. It's you he's after.'

The incoming rowing boat was so close that they could hear the soft, plashing sound of the strokes that brought it in. Behind, circling like a sheep-dog rounding up a stray lamb, came the motor-boat.

The rower, too, had heard the stones rolling from Una's fall. The strokes ceased. He hung on his oars, motionless, hesitating. 'What *is* all this?' demanded an aggrieved voice out of the darkness, in good English. 'Do you shoot strangers around these parts?'

The shock of astonishment stiffened them where they stood, and left them without breath to answer. The motor-boat, its engine stopped, closed in gently and lay clear of the oars, rippling softly alongside. Geestler's voice ordered, in his correct English: 'You will please come ashore.'

'Like hell I will!' said the invisible young man, but without rancour, as though curiosity already had the better of indignation, and he was only waiting to be asked nicely. 'Give me one good reason!'

'I really think you'd better,' said Lucas, with an effort dragging himself out of his stupor of surprise. 'The two gentlemen in the boat beside you are police officers.'

'Police officers?' Consternation and curiosity fought it out pretty evenly this time. 'What's the charge? Disturbing the peace?'

'Row to the jetty,' said Geestler patiently.

The young man hesitated for a moment, and then dipped his oars with a sigh and brought the boat about, nosing gingerly out of the arms of rock. There was no means of getting away from them. They edged him in watchfully to the jetty, and Schwalbe hopped ashore by the second flight of steps to receive him firmly by the arm as he stepped out of the boat. He bridled at that, but he didn't resist, even when Geestler made the boat fast in a hurry and sprang to take possession of his other arm. He was not seriously disturbed, only a little ruffled and more than a little intrigued.

'I'm not armed,' he assured them meekly, submitting to the inspection of quick and determined hands that went through his pockets without ceremony. 'Not unless you count my horn. And you be careful with that, it's my living you've got there. Anyhow,' he added in an injured voice, 'I can't have been as bad as all that. You didn't have to call out the militia.'

He was taking stock of his captors as well as he could in the darkness, and he had not missed the approaching shapes of the two girls, picking their way back with Lucas along the rocks. He watched them come closer, and was aware that they were examining him with equally intent interest. Some of the tension ebbed out of him.

'Now if *you'd* asked me to come ashore,' he said approvingly, eyeing Una's slender fairness, 'I'd have come like a shot at the first time of asking.'

'There's no occasion for impudence,' said Lucas sharply.

'There's been precious little for politeness yet, that I can see,' retorted the prisoner reasonably. 'But actually I intended a compliment. Well, I'm here. What happens next?'

'Come up to the house,' said Geestler. 'We'd like a talk with you.'

They kept their hold on him all the way back up the great staircases, but he stepped out willingly, so engrossed with the trim rear view of Una mounting before him that once he missed his footing on the broken stones, and had to be held up by his guards. He massaged a stubbed toe against his other calf, and finished the climb with at least half an eye on its hazards. They brought him into the lighted salon and closed the door, and Schwalbe set his chair against it, in case the prisoner should repent of his complacency and make a break for liberty.

Seen now in the revealing light of Herr Graf's chandelier, the horn-player was discovered to be a quite ordinary-looking young man of medium height and tawny colouring, lightly built, and attired in shabby grey slacks and a bulky fisher-knit sweater in a bright shade of corn-yellow. A thick crop of almost equally yellow hair, somewhat ruffled by his exertions and his handling, shed a long lock over one eye, and a bright, speculative eye it was, blue and roving. He accepted the chair Lucas rather helplessly offered him, and stared back steadily at all the thoughtful, baffled faces that contemplated and assessed him.

He can't be the one, thought Una. He hasn't done or said a single suspicious thing yet since they caught him. And yet the real Valentine would want to look and sound just like this, if he had to face them before he was ready. Perhaps he hadn't known the police would be here. And what was he doing rowing round the island, playing music almost nobody here could possibly know?

Lucas wasn't sure, either; his face was a study in doubt. 'I'm sorry,' he said constrainedly, 'but this is necessary. These officers will have to ask you to account for yourself. But if you can do so, of course – satisfactorily . . .'

'Why?' asked the boy pointblank, exchanging a hesitant grin for a sudden frown. 'Has there been a crime committed here?'

'Not yet,' said Lucas with a wry smile, and walked away across the room and left him to Geestler.

'Your name, please?'

'You've got my passport. You took it out of my pocket. And when you've done with it, by the way, I'd like it back.'

There was no doubt about it, the passport in Geestler's hands was British. Not new, rather grubby from being carried around a good deal. He studied the particulars in it carefully, thumbed through the pages and examined the many stamps in it.

'You are Michael Bracé? Of Cobham, in England?'

'That's right. Mike to my friends. But *you*,' he said sweetly, 'may call me Mr Brace.'

'By profession a musician?'

'Yes. Horn. Anything that blows, actually, but the horn's my real weapon. Well, I take it you heard me. May I smoke, please?'

'Spoil your wind,' said Lucas disapprovingly. But he offered him the box of cigarettes from the table, and then his lighter.

The boy flashed a startled glance into his face, and looked mildly encouraged. 'I don't, much, you know. Are you a musician yourself?'

'Of sorts,' said Lucas.

'Did you like that stuff I was tearing off, out there?' The voice had lost its defensive brashness; it warmed into ardour with engaging suddenness. 'Isn't it superb? Hell to play, but stunning if you can bring it off. I thought I was doing pretty well with it tonight, until you sent the marines. If I could write for the horn like that . . .'

Lucas turned his back with an abruptness which the young man obviously misinterpreted. He flushed and drew back, his ruffled, tawny brows drawing together in offence at the supposed rebuff. He really doesn't know, thought Una, relieved. He genuinely loves the music, and doesn't even know what Lu looks like. Valentine would certainly have known. There were photographs, even if Lu did shirk the camera. In concert programmes, in arts pages, on record sleeves. He isn't the one, she thought, and her heart rose like a bird, though she had no idea why.

'Have you been in Gries-am-See before?' Geestler pursued.

'No. I came here two weeks ago, that's the first time I'd seen the place.'

'What was your purpose in coming here?'

'To get a job. What else? I heard in Innsbruck that they were taking on extra players for the festival. I'm good enough to keep up with a small-town orchestra, any time. I thought it was worth a try. And I got in. Actually,' he said critically, 'they're not at all bad.'

'Then you had an audition with the director. When?'

The boy supplied day and hour cheerfully, facts which could very easily and quickly be checked.

'And you are lodging – where?'

'Frau Felbermayer, fifteen, Kirchgasse.' No hesitation there, and no reluctance. Geestler nodded contentedly, more than satisfied, for this was all too transparently verifiable to be false. Mr Brace's presence and business in Gries appeared to be eminently respectable, even if his habits were rather puzzling. For the only thing left unexplained was what he was doing in a rowing-boat off the Himmelhof at eleven o'clock at night, horn and all.

'I was getting in a little quiet practice,' said the boy, grinning. 'Out of earshot of the town, I hope. Out of reach, anyhow. I'll tell you. It's like this – three days ago the leading horn player went down with a feverish condition of the throat, some sort of bug he's picked up. And I stepped into his shoes. I know, I couldn't believe it, either, but you've only to ask old Seligmann, he'll tell you. Well, it isn't every day I get the chance to play music like that, I want to make a good job of it. A substitute's always got to be on his toes. But I can't sit around in the park blasting out what everybody in Gries is going to be paying to hear next week, can I? I reckoned there'd be room enough for me on the lake, if I left it until dark. Over the water it sounds good, too.'

He looked up and caught the full, delighted glance of Una's grey eyes, and it dazzled him. 'Did *you* like it?' he asked, hesitant on the edge of deliberate impudence, and recoiling into honest appeal.

'We all did,' Una admitted. 'But it certainly surprised us.'

'And your previous movements, please,' pursued

Geestler doggedly. 'You came to Gries from Innsbruck. How long were you there? You entered Austria more than three months ago.'

'That's right, I came . . .'

At that moment the telephone rang. The sound of the bell was enough, at this hour, to charge the air with an instant tension that stopped Mike Brace in mid-sentence, glancing from face to face. He remained silent because Crista had reached over quickly and picked up the instrument.

She turned to Lucas with a reassuring smile. 'Herr Wehrle for you, Mr Corinth.'

The casual utterance of the name closed Mike Brace's mouth like the spring of a trap. He cast one startled glance at the great man, and thereafter eyed him only furtively, in sidelong flashes of cagey blue eyes. Lucas, with the receiver at his ear, noticed nothing, intent on the deep voice at the other end of the line.

'Forgive me if I disturbed you. I wanted only to check once again that all is well there. Nothing further has developed? After this last incident . . . Everything is quiet there?'

'It is now,' said Lucas, briefly smiling. With the boy's ears stretched to pick up every clue – as they must be, considering his situation, if he was human – this was no time to make detailed reports. 'Herr Geestler will probably be giving you a call a little later – if you'll be still available for a while?'

'I shall indeed. I'll expect his call. That means something more has happened.'

'Nothing to keep any of us awake,' said Lucas. 'No trouble.'

'I take your word for it. Since I can talk more freely than apparently you can at the moment,' said Wehrle, 'you may like to know how far things have progressed. Frau Gelder did not return to her family when she left Gries. For a while they seem to have heard from her from Freistadt, we're following that up now. Both her parents are dead, it may take a few days to pick up the trail. But if she's alive we'll find her. Her son we'll certainly find – we've good reason to know he's alive. Keep your landward windows well covered when the lights are on, Mr Corinth. Better if the town doesn't find out too soon that the Himmelhof is occupied. It can't be kept secret for ever.'

'We hope,' said Lucas drily, 'that won't be necessary.'

'We hope not. Lock everything that will lock, and tell Hugo, when the time's right, that I'm waiting. Goodnight, Mr Corinth!'

'Goodnight!' Lucas laid the receiver in its rest. 'I beg your pardon! Please go on.'

'I was waiting,' said Geestler imperturbably, 'for our friend to give me details of his former movements in Austria, and his undertaking not to leave Gries.'

'You think I would,' said Mike, 'until this festival ends? Why should I quit a good job when I've found one?'

'No reason, Mr Brace, unless you have something on your conscience, of course. Give me particulars that can be checked for the whole time since you entered the country, and you may go back to the town and go to bed. What were you doing in Innsbruck? And where were you before that?'

The young man frowned down at his dwindling cigarette, patently considered his reply with some dour care, and then said in a flat voice: 'I'm sorry, but that's my business.'

'Once we have checked, so it can be. We're interested only in excising you from any enquiries that concern us. But that needs co-operation from you. You've been amenable until now, why this change?'

'I get stubborn,' said Mike, 'when pushed. I've given you fair answers, but that's far enough. I'm not saying another word.'

Puzzled and concerned, for after all this boy was a

very considerable musician, Lucas said warmly: 'Mr Brace, Frau Felbermayer needs her peace of mind – you'll be scolded for staying out too late as it is! – and Herr Geestler needs merely a few dates and addresses he can verify, and everyone will be happy. So why turn obstinate now, after being so admirably friendly? Not everyone would have taken it in such good part. Don't spoil your record now!'

It must be that marvellous high work on the horn, Una thought, touched and amused. Lu doesn't always go to the trouble to charm the young. If only this boy could realise it, he has him tamed already. She saw the slightly dazed, childishly gratified glance that was flashed upwards into Lu's face almost too quickly to be registered. She also saw the wide, candid mouth suppress its dazzled smile and set into even more obstinate determination. She had almost added her own persuasions, but she thought philosophically: If he won't for Lu, he won't for me!

'I'm sorry!' said Michael. 'I've shut up shop for the night.'

'I warn you,' said Geestler with a shrug, 'if you refuse to answer I shall have no choice but to keep you here until morning. I can't send you ashore now to check your story, I simply haven't the man-power. Supply all the details I'm asking for, and you can go. Refuse them, and you'll have to stay here until morning.'

'I've slept in worse places,' Mike Brace admitted, and the irrepressible grin surfaced for a moment, and again submerged. He looked round appreciatively at the regal absurdities of the Himmelhof, and the dazed look reappeared. 'They really *lived* like this?'

'A handful did,' said Lucas tartly. 'The rest slaved for a bare existence, as usual. Don't be silly, child! Trot out your credentials like a sensible fellow, and we'll put you ashore by motor-boat, and tow your boat back to town tomorrow.'

'I'm sorry!' he said, with every appearance of

meaning it, 'but no deal. I've stopped talking. You may as well accept that, because I mean it.'

'Very well,' said Geestler grimly. 'If you change your mind, let us know. We'll leave you within earshot, just in case. Take him along to the first empty room, Richard, the one with the sheer drop under the window. Lock him in.'

'May I have my horn?' asked Michael, too meekly.

'On the whole,' said Lucas, catching the irresponsible glint in the blue eye, 'I think not. Some members of this household may want to sleep. And I don't think any lullabies will be needed.'

'Impossible!' said Lucas firmly. 'The passport is undoubtedly genuine, and the boy is unquestionably British, and almost certainly exactly what he says he is. He can't be Valentine Gelder.'

'I agree. So does my chief. But don't forget this man has been in Austria three months, and refuses to tell us anything about his moves until he came to Gries. It is by no means impossible that he has been in contact with Gelder, and is being used by him now to sound out the approaches to this house. His connection with the orchestra may be for the same purpose. It is a way of getting close to you. If he had nothing to hide he would answer questions.'

'He's an extremely able musician, as we've heard for ourselves, and he wanted a job. I don't feel we need any better reasons than that for his applying for an audition. After all, this festival has been widely advertised, and musical openings don't grow on trees anywhere. I don't deny,' said Lucas ruefully, 'he may well have *something* to hide. Which of us hasn't? But criminal? – I doubt it! And certainly not as accomplice to Valentine Gelder.'

It was past midnight, and they had argued back and forth over the same ground twice already, since the boy had been hustled away, and Dieter Wehrle, fully informed and to a large extent reassured, had approved his lieutenant's proceedings and left the case of Michael Brace to his discretion. Lucas looked up at Crista Lohr, sitting withdrawn into the background as she always did, seeming to be at once among them and apart from them, her unsmiling quietness wrapped round her like a veil. When he caught her eyes they looked back at him with a shining gravity.

'What do *you* think, Miss Lohr?'

He was surprised himself that he had appealed to her. He had grown so accustomed to having her there close to him that he could no longer go on looking upon her simply as a piece of office equipment, without opinions. It began to annoy him that she should seem to be called into positive life only by the telephone, or an entry in her duty diary. Sometimes he even wanted her silence to be broken merely because the voice that emerged was so serious and warm; like her eyes, despite their determined aloofness.

'I think,' she said, after a moment's hesitation, and very gravely, 'that Valentine Gelder would not take an accomplice. I think he would not involve anyone but himself.'

'And I agree with you entirely,' said Lucas warmly. 'An opponent punctilious enough to issue his challenges publicly and confirm them privately, as he's done, isn't the man to hire casual labour to help him out, or to entangle his friends, either. Whatever he means to do, I believe he intends this clash to be single combat – man to man.'

'Nevertheless,' said Geestler firmly, 'I can't take any chances. If the young man had provided the details of his movements, I should have felt justified in letting him go back to his lodgings, though I should also have called my chief and seen to it that he was kept under observation until his story is checked. Since he apparently has something he feels compelled to hide, I cannot do anything else but hold him here until he can be escorted back to the town tomorrow, and his credentials tested. His presence here still seems to me suspicious.'

'Musically,' said Lucas with a faint smile, 'it's logical enough. Can you imagine practising the horn in a furnished room in the Kirchgasse? But I suppose sleeping overnight here won't do him any harm.' He rose, threading his fingers wearily through his hair, and looked at his watch. 'Lord, it's tomorrow already, I see!'

'Heut' oder Morgen!' Today or tomorrow. If Valentine kept strictly and successfully to his time-table, this very day they would know.

'Time I was in bed,' he said. 'Time we were all in bed. Whatever else happens, I've got a rehearsal this afternoon.'

'You can sleep in peace, Richard and I will be keeping watch in turns. But behind locked doors,' said Geestler drily, 'if you please.'

Lucas went out along the colonnade to his own room, and the other young man, patrolling the terrace below, gave him a quick smile and an airy salute in passing. Richard Schwalbe, the 'dark swallow'. Valentine had been dark, that he had not forgotten, dark and lean, like this one. Gay and yet taciturn, like this one. Did Wehrle know the antecedents of all his young men, back to their fathers and grandfathers?

The trouble with his situation, he thought, closing the door of his room behind him, and remembering for Geestler's sake rather than his own to turn the key in the lock, was that one began to peer into the face of every young man one met, looking for an enemy. At first with understandable wariness, even fear. But to some degree that seemed to be passing. He thought the time might even come when he would be scrutinising the young faces he encountered just as intently, looking for a friend, since he would by that time be looking not merely for the physical likeness of Valentine, but for his flesh and blood and the inheritor of his mind, a second Valentine. What did one say to such a match, such an opponent, on recognition?

He had brought Mike Brace's horn away with him into this locked sanctuary, unconsciously making it a duty to take care of another man's treasure as he would of his own. It had no case here, that must be in the boat, he supposed. They hadn't given the boy much time to think of details like that, the least Lucas could do was to make himself responsible. He ran a finger round the bell, and ran a finger-nail against its rim, drawing a small, rounded note of music.

At least he had heard that death-song played superlatively, and not even in innocence of its difficulties, as heaven-protected idiots skate happily immune over tissue-thin ice. No, the boy knew what he had done, knew what he meant to do. Somewhere at the back of a mind too young and blithe to brood about it, he had even grasped the significance of those cries which were not of defiance, not of heroic resolution, not of superhuman welcome to death and glory, but something much stranger and dual: the passionate protest of an ordinary, life-loving creature resisting and rejecting death with all his force, and at the same time the involuntary cry of self-realisation and wonder, as he found himself moving implacably, not away from it, but towards it.

Half-asleep, Lucas thought: I'm glad I was never a hero. They don't even know how much goes by them unrecognised!

CHAPTER EIGHT

Una waited until everything was silent, sitting fully-dressed on her bed. She was glad now that Crista, after her self-effacing fashion, had taken it for granted she should not presume to share this room, though there were two beds in it. More surprising was that she herself had not overruled these scrupulous arrangements; perhaps because she did not care to give the impression that she needed company for reassurance in this situation, perhaps because of a lingering doubt whether Crista did not, in reality, prefer to be alone. Now it suited her very well that she occupied, in splendid isolation, the last of the rooms prepared for their accommodation, next to the first of the long sequence that were empty – though to judge by the general state of the house it would be empty only of modern amenities, otherwise rather over-furnished than under. In the room next door to hers the young man called Mike Brace was incarcerated.

She had already examined the outlook from her window, earlier in the evening, and the curve of the outer wall turned the neighbouring window some-what away from her own. Better, probably, from the room on the other side, which was smaller, and less affected by the alignment of the wing. There, too, she would be further away from her father and Crista, who, she hoped, were already sleeping.

Though she did not herself believe in it, it was still a possibility that this supposedly English boy somehow had access to papers forged with sufficient expertise to make him whatever he wanted to be. It was even a possibility – stretching drama to its limit, and why not, when they were operating so near the limit already? – that he was Valentine Gelder. How can you find out for certain? Ask him a question like that, and whatever the truth, he must and will say no, of course he isn't. Ask him if he knows the name, and whatever he answers, the tone of his voice may have something to say. But Una wanted to talk to him, whether he was or not. He was a captive audience now, he would have to listen. If he was sane, he could be convinced; and if she could manage to convince him, there was everything to gain. For him, as well as for Lucas.

And if, as she felt in her bones, he wasn't Valentine? What was there to lose, in that case? And perhaps an ally to gain. They could do with genuine allies.

She unlocked the door of her room cautiously, bracing her left hand over her right to ease the turning of the key. There was almost no sound. When it was done she opened the door a crack, and again listened, but everything was silent. She slipped out into the corridor, taking the key with her, felt her way in the faintly luminous darkness past the one door between, and let herself into the room she had chosen, shutting herself in silently.

The lambent light from the water, still fed with a few fixed stars from the distant shore, lanced in through the window and trembled across the painted ceiling. Una groped her way between draped furniture that smelled of satin upholstery, and wood-gilt, and dust. The window gave easily to her hand, and she looked out over the rocky drop below, not sheer but descending in broken ledges and spiky pinnacles towards the water. She didn't know whether she would be able to reach the window of the room next door, or whether she would have to call to him. If she did, would he hear? Without waking anyone else? If there was a bed in there he might be fast asleep, with the window half-closed against the night, and tired young men sleep soundly.

She need not have worried. As soon as she leaned out and looked along the peeling outer wall to the next window on her right, she saw that he was there, leaning on his folded arms, contemplating the distant and inaccessible prospect of Gries, now reduced to a few scattered lights on the far shore. She pushed the window wide, and leaned out on a level with him, kneeling as he must be kneeling; and at the slight sound she made he looked round sharply, his head braced warily.

'Oh!' he said blankly. 'It's you.' And he smiled; even in the dark it was a wide, bright smile. 'Hullo!' he said. 'Nice to see you again so soon.'

'I want to talk to you,' said Una, just above a whisper.

'Nothing I'd like better. I wish you'd begin,' he said plaintively, 'by telling me what all this is about. What am I supposed to have done, and to whom, and how does Lucas Corinth figure in it? If he really is Lucas Corinth?'

'He is,' she said. 'He's my father.' She was wondering how to set about this, and how much of what seemed crystal truth about this young man could safely be believed. 'Didn't you really know, until Crista called him by his name?'

'No, of course I didn't. Why should I? I suppose I must have seen pictures of him sometimes, but not all that often, and he didn't strike me as much like them, even now. And anyhow, why should I expect to find him here? I didn't know there was anyone here. And I thought he was staying at the Grand. I must have come in fairly close before your house lights were on – they didn't show, anyhow, or I wouldn't have come any nearer. I wasn't aiming to annoy anybody.' The slight smart of offence in his voice was wonderfully convincing; if it had been acted, it might have been overdone. This was a sunny soul, he didn't hold anything against anybody for long, and he was given to finding awkward situations also very funny. What was funny, at this moment, about being Valentine Gelder? Could one carry what he was carrying, and laugh?

'Do you mean to say,' she demanded in the same forceful undertone, 'that you haven't even read yesterday's papers? I didn't think there was anyone in Gries by this time who didn't know all about it.'

'About *what*? No, I didn't buy a paper yesterday. Or all the week, for that matter. To tell you the truth,' he said in a burst of candour, 'I've got just enough money to keep me in thinnish meals until I draw my next pay. Etceteras like drinks and papers are out. So are cigarettes, that's why I couldn't resist scrounging one from your dad just now. So no, I don't know what the hell this is all about. So suppose you tell me.'

'I will,' she said. 'The truth and the whole truth. And do something for me, because believe me, I'm not playing games. Even if your name isn't Michael Brace, and you're not as innocent as you make out, and even if you don't regard me as an unbiased reporter, will you at least, for God's sake, *go on listening*, and entertain, just as a remote possibility, the idea that what I'm telling you *may* be true? That's all I'm asking.'

She had shaken him clean out of any desire to laugh, or to take this matter, whatever it might be, lightly. He was silent for a long moment, staring at her, leaning well out to his left to see her more closely and search her face more earnestly. They were straining towards each other, in fact, like imprisoned lovers trying to embrace, and the rest of the world had receded into the farthest recesses of the night, leaving them alone.

'Look,' he said gently and slowly, 'are you in some kind of trouble? You and your old man? I do know about him – a bit – what everybody knows. I shouldn't like anything to go wrong now. I mean, of course, very much for my own sake, now I've got my hands on this plum, but hell, not for his sake, either. Well, it's kind of a feudal relationship, if you know what I mean. I'm his man.'

Una thought, dazedly, that music had a lot to answer for. How powerful the mediaeval element in her father's writing must be, to climb out of its grave, brush past the bitter intent that denied it, and still clamp Lucas's hands over this young man's hands, and exact a kind of fealty. Even if he didn't mean it quite literally – as how could he? – even so it was a miracle. Lu had judged, isolated, subjected to the bitter light of human reason all those myths of hero- ism and loyalty and self-sacrifice, and his strictures were just and justified, and seen to be so, and yet this indestructible value rose again valid as ever. Mike Brace might be quite capable of laughing at it, but it was still significant to him, and he was just as likely to act on it.

'You know about his wartime record, too?' she said. 'When he was just a boy?'

'Yes, I know. They wrote it all up in the festival hand-out, the one that brought me here.'

He was, of course, too young to have known, otherwise. And he was exactly who and what he repre- sented himself to be; by then she was certain of that. In a sense there was now no need to tell him anything, for what could he do in the matter, and what need was there now to convince him of anything? All the same, she took a deep breath, and told him everything, from the first unexplained telephone call, through the sud- den eruption of the whole struggle into the ungentle light of day, and of public controversy, to this refuge at the Himmelhof, and the mystery and threat of the horn-calls from the water. On the way to this ending she had also told him, briefly but faithfully, the story according to Lucas.

When she stopped talking there was a brief and thoughtful silence. Then he said intently:

'So when I showed up, I was cast for this fellow Gelder?'

'You came just after that warning. And you came playing that horn music – the death music. Music nobody but the orchestra should have known. And ominous in the circumstances. You can see why they were suspicious. And then refusing to say where you'd been and what you'd been doing before you came to Gries. Why *did* you? If you'd told them, they were ready to let you go. You had them convinced, until you clammed up so suddenly about your movements.'

'I had my reasons,' said the young man sombrely, and brooded a moment in his window, chin on crossed wrists. 'In a few days, if all goes well, I could tell you. But nothing to do with any Valentine Gelder.'

'No,' she agreed, 'I know that now.'

'In a way, I'm even sorry. If I were him, I'd give you best and swear off the whole thing, like a shot. But I'm just Mike Brace. That's not much immediate help, I'm afraid.'

'I didn't expect you,' she owned with a sigh, 'to be able to help. I just thought that if you *were* . . . Well, it was an opportunity to talk to you, to try to make you see reason. It's nice,' she said truthfully, 'even that Mike Brace believes me.'

'Oh, I believe you, all right. Trouble is that we haven't got any way of shanghai-ing this Valentine, and making him see sense. I suppose,' he said, 'they are trying to find him?'

'Every young man who comes near, and looks anywhere around twenty-seven, is suspect. Yes, they're trying. But the mother left here and didn't go back to her parents in Linz, and nobody knows where she vanished to. It takes time. And I'm not sure that we're dealing with an ineffective romantic. I don't think we have time.'

'Have you thought of the other way? Find the man

your dad spoke to at the Filsertal gate. The man he gave the legitimation to. That would be even more effective, because that would *prove* he's telling the truth.'

'After all these years? He may be dead long ago. But yes, they've got that in mind, too.'

'You mustn't think like that. Equally he may be alive. Your dad put him at around forty then, that would make him in his late sixties now. But that's not senile. Not even old, for a Tyrolese.'

'But look how many people died in the war.' She was thinking, bitterly, of Willi Bruchmann.

'Our man was too old to get dragged into that automatically, and too wily, if he was a travelling man. And nobody was rushing armies up and down the Silvretta, or bothered to bomb Vesulspitze. He may very well be still alive, and still running round from fair to fair, if he was what your father took him to be. I'm a connoisseur of travelling men, I'm a bit of one myself. You'd be surprised what regular habits they have. You could set your watch by some of the gypsies. Tell me about him again. Tell me every word your father said, when he was trying to remember for the police.'

At first she had been no more than comforted and touched by his interest, now she was beginning to take heart from it, almost against her judgment, even to believe that if this young man set out to find a single elderly vagabond in the whole of Austria he would have the cheek and the luck to succeed. She shut her eyes, the better to concentrate, and went over the remembered details yet once again. The pitch darkness in the woods, the tree that stirred and became a man, the age, the shape, the smell of him, the way he turned his head side-long to hide his face, the harsh detail of what he had heard while he froze into immobility.

'Your old man noticed a good deal,' said Mike, impressed.

'You daren't miss anything when your life depends on it. And those things you don't forget.'

'No, I don't suppose you do,' he said feelingly. 'Let's hope that goes double, even after twenty-eight years. There can't have been many nights like that in the other fellow's life, either. And you do know, don't you, that if this chap really was the travelling kind, whether he belonged to one of the shows or was a lone camp-follower, he may very well be in Gries right now?'

'The police have thought of that, too. They're looking for him at the fairground. But surely he'd have come forward when he read the account in the papers,' she objected. 'Even if he's still alive, and still on the road, there are fairs at the other end of Austria, too.'

'There are, and I know it's a long chance, but long chances are all you've got. You know what?' said Mike seriously, watching her face in the soft, lambent light. 'You've given me an idea. It may not pay off, but it's worth a try. If I'm right, our man's range may turn out to be strictly local, probably never beyond the Tyrol. And like me, he doesn't read the papers. I'll tell you something! The first three nights I spent in Gries, even after I got taken on with the orchestra, I slept rough on the fairground, and did a few jobs around the shows during the day. I hadn't any money for a room until I got my first pay, and I've lived that way before, when pushed. I met acquaintances I've made the other side of the Arlberg, and some from further afield still, and where I don't know my way around, and can't talk fast enough, they do, and they can. And it looks,' he said thoughtfully, 'as though I'd better get back there just as soon as I can, and not hang around until morning. If today is – maybe – all we've got.'

She hardly noticed that 'you, had suddenly changed to 'we'. There had been nothing deliberate about his self-election, it was as direct and impulsive as everything he did.

Torn between eagerness and doubt, she said: 'But you can't. They won't let you go now.'

'They will if I come clean. They said so.'

'But you said you had reasons – I mean, if there are things you don't want the police to know about you . . . It's awfully good of you, but how can I let you . . .'

'The police?' he said, surprised. 'Don't you worry, I'm not a wanted man – not any more. No, it was something quite different I was aiming to keep dark, and it doesn't matter all that much now, not by comparison with this.' He rose from his knees, and tugged down his sweater like a man preparing for action. 'Look, it may not even matter at all, if . . . Is your old man still there?'

'No, he went to bed some time before I came in here. I hope he's asleep. He needs it.'

'That makes it easy,' he said with satisfaction. 'Look, you can do us all a favour. Well, I *hope* it'll turn out a favour! Go find that copper who was doing the talking, and tell him I'm suitably chastened, and knocked on the wall to let somebody know I wanted out, and was ready to talk. That *is* you in the room the other side of me? And rub it well into him that your old man mustn't be disturbed, because he needs all the rest he can get. OK? And then you go to bed, and leave the rest to me. I've got a hunch, and Mike's hunches always pay off. One of 'em brought me to Gries, and that wasn't any dud, you'll admit. Try not to worry. I'll be back. And with a lot of luck, not alone. You go get your beauty sleep. Not that you need any more help from nature,' he said with a candid grin, 'she went to town on you in the first place. Do you know I still don't even know your name?'

'It's Una,' she said. He generated a wind of energy that was bidding fair to blow her off her feet.

'Then I'll see you at rehearsal. OK? And goodnight – Una!'

'Goodnight, Mike!'

He had already vanished from the window when impulsively she called him back.

'Mike, I thought you might like to know . . . I wouldn't worry about that horn part, if I were you. After you'd gone he called you an extremely able musician. He never says more than he means, usually not so much.'

'No!' breathed Mike, struck mute for a moment. 'No kidding, he really said that? You wouldn't pull my leg, would you?'

'I wouldn't. And he did.'

Mike hung from his window entranced for a moment. His face gradually broke into an incandescent grin. 'You know what?' he said then. 'If I could reach that far I'd kiss you, Una Corinth!'

She measured the distance between the windows with a speculative eye, and let herself go with the gale. 'I could come part way to meet you,' she offered.

But all they could manage, when they stretched out towards each other along the cool, rough wall, was a brief clasping of fingertips.

CHAPTER NINE

Lucas awoke to the smell of fresh coffee, and the scintillating light of the morning sun reflected from the lake water into his gold and white room. He bathed and dressed, and went out into the colonnade, and walked to the edge of the terrace, without so much as thinking of the possible lurker in the bushes below, or the weathered demi-god dislodged from the cornice. He had slept well, and awakened early, and the apparition of the Silvretta peaks, flushed aloft with the dawn like rose-coloured diamonds, and afloat below in a mist as blue as hyacinths, made his heart soar as if this were the first, original, ecstatic day of the world – of *his* world – instead of the last.

Richard Schwalbe was patrolling the tiers of gardens below him, probing bushes, but perfunctorily, as though he did not quite believe in his task. He was whistling, and his step was a dance step. When he looked up and saw Lucas above him, he waved a hand – definitely less of a salute than a wave this time – and called a good-morning. He was laughing. He laughed a great deal, not at any private joke, but out of some joyous animal exuberance. Disinclination to words turned him naturally to such outlets as whistling, and laughter, and light, balletic gesture.

'I hope,' called Lucas, dazzled by so much energy, 'you were able to get some sleep?'

'Two hours,' said the young man cheerfully. 'It's enough. And you, sir? You slept well?'

'Thank you, I did. Is Herr Geestler anywhere about?' He was thinking of the prisoner still locked in one of the dust-sheeted rooms. He hoped that at least there had been a bed in it.

'Hugo went down to the jetty. A boat came in with the mail and the newspapers. He'll be on his way up by now. Oh, the boat signalled and was identified, of course, everything is in order. It was a quiet night,' he said blithely, and moved on along the terrace until the overgrown shrubs hid him from sight.

The air was like iced wine, and the sky above the island, still tinted with the dawn, was so remote and delicate a lilac shade that it faded at the zenith into the colourlessness of space. In a little while the valiant blue would emerge, to deepen and deepen into noon's incredible peacock hue. Now everything was vapour, pallor and sparkle, everything tinkled like frost, though the sun was already warming the stones. Lucas had never felt more alive, or valued living more.

Geestler, coming up the gap-toothed staircases, frowned at the sight of his charge standing thus vulnerably in the full sunlight, visible from every side.

'You should go in, or at least keep within the precinct. I'm sorry, but you know the need.' He reproached rather than ordered, and Lucas felt guilty rather than threatened. But he knew he was not yet out of reach of fear; it was merely that the startling beauty of those distant peaks made him forget.

'Your colleague has just vetted all these levels,' he said defensively, 'and you've come up from the shore, this seemed the best time for a breather. Shouldn't we set our young guest free, too? I'm afraid he may have spent a rather wretched night, at least we can offer him breakfast.'

Geestler reshuffled the packages in his hands, and for one moment looked slightly deprecating. His was a rocky, conscientious young face, it took any hesitancy hard.

'This young Englishman,' he said, 'after you had

retired, had second thoughts about his situation, Mr
Corinth. I think you won't disapprove. He asked to
be released, and voluntarily gave us a complete
account of his movements in Austria since he entered.
He was candour itself. He offered every safeguard we
could require, and there'll be no difficulty in keeping
a watch on him. So I felt justified in allowing him to
leave, as he wished.'

'You got the statement you wanted?' said Lucas,
astonished.

'In complete detail, yes.'

'And you let the poor kid row back to Gries? In the
middle of the night?'

Geestler smiled. 'It was not so late, not long after
you retired. But in fact I had Richard tow him across
with the motor-boat. A matter of ten minutes. He
would be back at his lodgings soon after one o'clock.
He has to be ready for rehearsal this afternoon, as you
have. It seemed a reasonable risk. As you said, quite
definitely he is not Valentine Gelder.'

'But I have his horn,' said Lucas, amused and dismayed. 'Why didn't you call me? Didn't he insist? He
must be feeling terribly aggrieved against me for the
whole episode. I wouldn't for the world have robbed
him.'

'Miss Corinth was most urgent that we should not
disturb you.'

'You mean my daughter was present?' He was more
and more at sea; so many things here, by night as by
day, were happening without any reference to him, as
though he had already passed out of existence.

'No, no, no! But Miss Corinth occupies the room
next to the one where we had put him. It seems that he
knocked on the wall, begged her to call me. She was
naturally anxious that we should not trouble you.
And the horn . . . Yes! Mr Brace agreed that you must
not be awakened. You will find he has left you a note.
And there are letters here, and the newspapers . . .'

'Take them in, please,' Lucas requested, shrinking

from the characteristic columnar black and white, pointed with red, of the press. 'I'll come in a few minutes. This,' he said, looking out at the world that composed itself into such a devastating shape at the south-western extreme of the Himmelsee, 'is so beautiful.'

He saw this young face – all the faces that surrounded him were so young, all of them hovered round that magical twenty-seventh year – quiver and respond, acknowledging and respecting what he felt. Geestler opened his lips to speak, and then after all closed them, having said nothing. He took his bundle of letters and papers, and went away quietly and almost stealthily into the house.

Crista was alone in the salon when Lucas entered. She had laid a small table for breakfast, for two people only, and was ready to pour coffee for him and bring in toast from the kitchen as soon as he appeared. There were flowers on the table, a few sprays cut from the overflowing shrubberies, and she had found some Mozart on the radio as subdued background music. He noticed, too, that she had folded the newspaper away under his letters, so that it should not clamour too blatantly for his attention and spoil his morning, and even mustered the letters themselves carefully, English and private ones first, so that he should be able to begin with normality, whatever vicious freaks might have to be faced later. This was going to be no comfortable day for him, but she was fending off its most hurtful edges as best she could.

On top of the whole pile was a single sheet of paper folded in half, pale blue notepaper from the writing-table beside the window. Lucas unfolded it with a smile, and read:

'Dear Mr Corinth,
      I have now satisfied the police of my bona fides, and they're letting me go back to Gries,

but I find I'm obliged to leave my horn behind.
We didn't want to wake you. Would you be so
kind as to bring it with you to rehearsal this
afternoon? I'm asking your man to bring up the
case from my boat when he gets back from
giving me a tow across.

Thank you!'

And the signature: Michael Brace. An unflowing,
schoolboy hand. Lucas doubted if his absent friends
got many bulletins from him, or his parents when he
was wandering. Supposing, of course, that he had any
parents living? Lucas had very little experience of
what motives drive the young across the world in
times of peace; he knew very acutely those impulsions
that do the same office for them in wartime.

The case was on one of the brocaded chairs by the
wall, as shabby and striking, and fully as assured, as
an infantry private quartered in a baroque church.
Scuffed black leather over blocked wood, rubbed raw
at the corners. Maybe his father had played the same
horn before him, maybe his grandfather, too. Horns
and trumpets have long, long lives. The Viking lurs
can still be blown, and the shattering brilliance of the
war trumpet from the Egyptian tomb must be one of
the most marvellous sounds ever recorded.

He laid the note gently on the table. Crista's eyes
followed it, and returned to his face. 'Herr Geestler
feels a little apologetic. But it was better not to wake
you.'

'Apologetic?' He was honestly puzzled for a
moment. 'Oh, for letting me be the young man's
errand-boy? Why not? It was on my account he was
inconvenienced in the first place. I'm glad to make
amends. Una isn't up yet?'

'Not yet.' She hesitated a moment, her fingers busy
rearranging a spray of flowering orange that had
tilted too far in the bowl. 'I don't know if you have
any plans for the morning. I know Herr Wehrle would

be grateful if you would stay on the island until it's necessary to go to the rehearsal. But as Miss Corinth hasn't seen the castle yet, I thought we might cross over a little earlier, and go to the other landing-stage on the point. I can have a car waiting there for us just as easily as at the town jetty.'

He turned to give her a sudden attentive look, remembering a number of little things that had preceded the flowers on the table, the delicate considerations of the music and the letters. He was alone with her. It was the first time, he realised, and it would surely last no more than a few minutes; and in any case time was potentially a scarce commodity for him. It was as well to say the things that ought to be said, quickly, simply, without hesitation. And one of them was due to her.

'You thought,' he said deliberately, 'that I would prefer not to arrive where the curious will be waiting to stare at me. That's what you mean. And you're quite right.'

Her eyes opened wide, but she had nothing to say.

'Crista, will you allow me to thank you for all you've done and are doing for me? Please believe that I know, almost better than you, how much it is, and I'm grateful for the intent even more than for the performance. You're kind, and you comfort me very much. You're also very discerning. You see in me a not very brave man who would like to run like a hare from curiosity and criticism, let alone condemnation. And you're right, I would like to. But I'm not going to. You've shown me what's due from me, and that's one more thing for which I'd like to thank you. I'll go ashore at the main jetty. And if Herr Graf has an open car free, as far as I'm concerned he can send that for me. Let them have a good look. It might help them to make up their minds – though God knows which way!'

He'd said more than he'd intended, he realised that. He'd hurt her instead of touching her lightly.

She had grown very pale, the colour ebbing even from her lips.

'I did not mean,' she began in a low and trembling voice, 'to suggest that you . . . that you are afraid . . .'

'Why not?' he said gently. 'It would be justified. I *am* afraid. But, curiously, not so afraid as I was.'

'It is my job,' she said, 'to make everything run smoothly for you, I am only trying to do that, as I undertook to do it. You have no right to – to . . . You make it sound as though I've insulted you!'

'Then I'm a clumsy fool,' he said, dismayed. 'I meant no such thing. God, no, you've done me more than justice.' He was terrified that there were tears gathering in the dark eyes. He took her hand very quickly, and lightly kissed the backs of the smooth young fingers that were so cold in his. 'You've helped me, not hurt me,' he said. 'Don't for God's sake, make me feel that I've hurt you, or I shall be miserable for the rest of my life.'

Crista turned her head aside, with a stiff, blind motion of pain and resistance, drew her hand away as though his touch burned, and went very quickly out of the room.

He stood where she had left him, shaken and chastened, wanting to go after her and make good whatever he had done wrong, but uneasily aware that he might make bad worse. And she had always been so aloof and contained! What had happened to her, within that shell of calm, while she had been caught up into his accidental circle of tension and strain? He should never have touched her. Where was the kindness in involving her more deeply, even with gratitude? Disgusted with his own clumsiness, he sat down to his coffee, but with his ears pricked for the soft click of her sandals returning. But when he looked up warily at the first light step in the corridor, it was Una who came in.

She looked round the room, noted his solitary

condition, and the fact that the table was laid for only two, and asked at once: 'Aren't the bodyguard eating with us this morning?'

'I rather think,' said Lucas, 'that they breakfasted before we were up. They both seem to be out on patrol at the moment.'

'And Crista? Oh, dear, she's done everything single-handed. I intended to be up in time to help.'

'Didn't you meet her? She went out only a few minutes ago. I think she must have breakfasted with the young men.'

'And what about the other young man?' Una asked. 'Aren't we going to feed him, too?'

She had not been sure until this moment whether she was going to tell Lucas what had passed in the night or not. It was the sight of his bent head and shadowed brow as he studied the letters that made up her mind for her. True, a draught of hope could do him nothing but good, provided it was well grounded; but how could she make her account, at second-hand, as convincing to him as the reality had, for some reason, been to her? She drew back from the difficulties of making long explanations which would explain nothing, but only create a tangle of minor doubts and annoyances, some of them – such as irritation that she should act independently with doubtful discretion – childish. Not petty – there was nothing petty about Lu – but yes, childish. His pattern of essentials had always been different from hers, and he would be seeing Mike Brace from quite a different viewpoint. Hope, too, could be double-edged. No, she would hold her hand, and wait for hope to become substance. Even if he knew, he could not help in any way whatever enterprise Mike had in mind.

'The bird's flown,' Lucas said with a faint smile, and handed her the note to read. 'Apparently he thought better of it, and decided to get himself off the hook. But he left a hostage behind.' He nodded towards the case on its brocaded throne. 'We have to 'take his horn with us to the hall this afternoon. Or rather,' he corrected himself, 'I have. No need for you to come to the rehearsal, you go off with Crista and have a look at the castle, and pick me up afterwards.'

Una refolded Mike's note with a private and almost invisible smile. 'No, I'm coming with you.'

He was surprised for a moment. Rehearsals usually bored her to extinction, and he knew it. Then he realised that she had now no intention of letting him out of her sight for a moment if she could help it. He offered her his warmest smile. 'Oh, come!' he said gently. 'I can't come to much harm in the company of the entire orchestra, can I?'

'I'm coming with you,' she said again, with such determination and finality that he didn't presume to argue further. But he did wonder, mildly and fleetingly, why she should flush so fiercely as she overruled him. Almost as though her loyalty was something to be ashamed of.

Crista reappeared to take down two letters for him, make the necessary telephone calls, supply Geestler and Schwalbe with more coffee at mid-morning, and help Una to cook an early lunch. She was perfectly composed and exactly as usual, trim and precise in her yellow linen suit, a girl of few words and scrupulously controlled actions. Her attentive but aloof attitude to Lucas had not changed at all. Clearly he was not to be made to pay for his morning indiscretion – though what had been indiscreet about it he still could not quite fathom – nor did she intend to take the slightest advantage of it.

It was an encouragement to him, rather than otherwise, that she should take him at his word. No more mention was made of landing at the castle jetty. It was to the main landing-stage of the town that Richard Schwalbe steered them in the motor-boat at half past one; and if the car that met them there was not an open car, that was doubtless due to Herr Graf's tender consideration for his own investment. On such a glorious day the lake-side promenade was crowded with strollers, shoppers and holiday-makers regaling themselves on beer and coffee and ice-cream at the pavement cafés. The beach was bright with bathers and children, the shore waters full of small craft. The whole of Gries, *en fête*, had come out into the sun.

Schwalbe made the boat fast, and the sunburned young man who was his relief dropped lightly down from the jetty as soon as the party was ashore. Another anonymous boy vaguely in those later twenties, another with eyes hidden by sun-glasses. But before nightfall Schwalbe would be back again after his rest. It was his assignment, he was detailed to stay with it to the end. Whatever that end might be.

Lucas walked with deliberate slowness between the strolling promenaders, refusing to hasten his steps when he saw that he was recognised. Heads turned, feet lagged, eyes rounded, people nudged one another and whispered, morning papers were turned hurriedly to confirm the identification. This was the man! This was the lion they were saying now was no lion, but a coward who ran to save his own skin and left his friend to die. Of course he denied it. But it was easy enough to say he had a witness, so long as it was the kind who couldn't possibly be produced.

Gries had not yet made up its mind what to believe. When it did, Lucas Corinth would soon find out which way it had decided. So would the concert offices. If the decision went the wrong way he might very well find himself boycotted, and the effect on Herr Graf's prospects and prestige, and the town's balance sheet, would be catastrophic. The July Festival might never recover from a blow like that.

In the harbour park the car waited for them, drawn as close to the stage as possible; and Lucas was well aware that on either side of them, as they crossed to it, strolled a policeman in plain clothes. No skin-fitting tee-shirts here, but loose cotton jackets adequate to cover the holsters of their guns. They sauntered, but kept station, looking very like all the middle-aged saunterers around them. He wondered if this large black limousine, slightly hearse-like already to his sardonic eye, had bullet-proof glass.

Crista sat beside the driver. Una settled herself beside Lucas in the back seat, her arm firm and warm against his, whether to comfort him or herself she hardly knew. They had never felt the need to be demonstrative, and could not begin now.

'I feel naked,' she said, watching the frieze of peering faces slide by on either side.

'So do I, but I'm getting used to the idea. After all, naked I came into the world, and naked . . .' He broke off there with a slightly distorted smile, realising where his tongue was leading him. 'Do you really want to come to this session? No need, you know. Once I'm delivered to the Town Hall nothing can happen to me, and you'll be picking me up again there afterwards.'

She shook her head. 'I'm coming.' Briefly she smiled; to herself, but he caught the fleeting brightness. It was true that usually rehearsals bored her. Unless you had some instrument to play, a personal flag to show and a personal fulfilment to win, all those maddening repetitions and snatches and insistent, punishing exercises, frequently getting more and more tired and cross, were a penance. Today she had private reasons for not expecting even to be bored by this one, and more urgent and equally private reasons for hoping for a more than musical gain from it. Though what could he have done in so few hours? What could he even have attempted, beyond what the police, with greater resources, were doing already, combing the fairground and questioning its habitués? Unless, of course, he really had recognised something, penetrated to some possibility, which everyone else had missed?

The car drove into the courtyard of the Town Hall,

under the foaming window-boxes and across the polished cobbles. Werner Seligmann was waiting in the vestibule to lead them to the hall where the orchestra was gathering, in the usual chaotic aviary noise of plucked strings, and tentative chords, and soft, blown notes from the brass, and loud general conversation by way of continuo. A high rostrum for Lucas, and a forest of music-stands and chairs; and all those faces turning towards the door as they entered, and the hush.

Only a momentary hush, for they were early, and a few players were still coming and making their way to their places. The chorus began again. Herr Seligmann wandered among the ranks with a hand at Lucas's elbow, presenting the leader, and the principal players of the sections.

'And our horn soloist . . .'

He looked round for him, as Una had been looking round, from her retirement in a quiet corner, ever since they had entered the room. She was nursing his horn in its case, her passport to him as soon as he should appear. Musicians on their non-public occasions are an untidy, casual, down-to-earth crowd, and there were so many of them here, and moving around so loosely, that it was difficult to be sure at first who was present and who was not. Yet she thought she would have been able to pick him out on the instant if he had been there. That yellow hair, and the corn-coloured sweater . . . No, he was not in the room. As Herr Seligmann had just discovered, to his consternation. He went on talking, with creditable delicacy, and one eye on the door. 'Your own countryman, Mr Corinth. At least, what I mean is that he is English.'

'So I've been hearing,' said Lucas.

'He came to us as an unknown quantity, of course, but he has turned out so well that when Müller went down with this throat infection we could do no other than put this boy in his place. You will see what you think of him. Personally I am enthusiastic. He lacks experience of course, but he is enormously gifted, and has excellent musical judgement. Confidence? – well – perhaps a little too much confidence, even! But he will learn.'

'In time,' said Lucas, rather drily but without any ill-humour, 'I hope he may even learn to be punctual.'

'I assure you it's unusual. He takes his music very seriously. There must be a reason. But I agree he is late. Perhaps you would like to begin without him.'

In her corner Una sat and wondered, as Seligmann presented the composer-conductor, and handed over his orchestra to Lucas's mercies. Was it possible that that boy had fooled her, after all? Had he really had something serious to hide, and taken the opportunity of skipping while they were lulled into believing him harmless? She couldn't believe it. Mike Brace was honest, and she was staking her own faith on him.

The rehearsal had been in progress for more than seven minutes, and Lucas was gradually warming into eagerness and animation, as he did with deceptive slowness on these first occasions. In the middle of a smooth, slow passage the door opened quietly but abruptly, and in the brief burst of invading sunlight the yellow head glowed. He exploded violently but silently into the room, and the door closed after him with a faint but distinct clap. Lucas looked up, and broke off operations with a flick of his baton.

Una had the horn out of its battered case before the silence washed to the back of the hall, and had slid softly round to the door and thrust it into Mike's hands. He gave her one startled but welcoming look, made a conspirator's face at her, and shot to his place, composing himself into an image of innocence all in one movement. He lifted the horn experimentally to his lips, and raised a wary blue eye to see how Lucas was taking it.

Where most people keep the rough edge of their tongues, Lucas kept a smooth cutting edge which could be more effective. He gazed back steadily at the delinquent, long enough to produce absolute silence.

'Would five pages give Mr Brace time to recover his breath?' he inquired with solicitous gentleness.

'I beg your pardon, sir,' Mike apologised engagingly, in very passable German to match the question, 'for turning up late. I was unavoidably delayed. It won't happen again.' And he cocked one cautious eye at Lucas, and affirmed brazenly, still panting: 'I'm quite ready to play.'

'Good, I'm glad to hear that. Then let's proceed now to the third part, shall we?' He located the bar, and with what Una privately considered unpardonable vindictiveness, took Mike at his word, driving them at a slightly exaggerated tempo – they might not realise it this time, but they would when he wasn't being bloody-minded – through the most fiendishly difficult passages he had ever written for the solo horn.

It went a little raggedly, but with mounting excitement and force. Honours were about even. Mike survived the ordeal without disgrace, though he emerged with heaving chest and damp forehead; and Lucas ended laughing. He kept his face straight, but Una knew when he was laughing. After that he settled down to the business in earnest, and let Mike Brace alone. And Una knew, if Mike did not – and she suspected he did – that Lucas was pleased with him.

She knew what she had taken on, coming to sit through this. He would work them and himself to death, and as soon as they were released all of them, Lucas included, would feel rather more than usually alive and refreshed, potent and creative. She was the one who had to endure what she could not share. Not yet, not until it flowered in performance. If, of course, it ever did! But it had to! Nobody on earth had the right to deprive the world of art, or its creator of his fulfilment, or its interpreters of theirs, which was equally valid.

Una played no instrument, had not perfect pitch, could not sing except as people sing for their own satisfaction. But she knew about music, and this was going well; Lucas was surprised and pleased at the material he had to work with, and they were responsive to him. When he burned up, he could set them both alight. And Roland's horn . . . There was a certain distraction of mind there, she thought, compensated for, sometimes too generously, by a wild lyricism which was not quite in the score. He was thinking of something else, parallel with his passionate thinking about what he was doing. His tone was lovely, pure and confident. Lu would teach him, at some happier and more peaceful time, how to discipline the imagination that drove it. But this was no fair test; his mind was divided. It was not musical arrogance that made him strain; he was drawing on all the resources he had in order to play, and reason, and plan all at the same time.

It ended at last, late, as it had begun. It was five o'clock before Lucas laid down the baton, and lifted a tired, perspiring face to his orchestra. Only then did she realise that he had been preparing the ground for someone else to take over, if this should be both his first and last rehearsal with them.

'Thank you, gentlemen, that's enough for today. I'm afraid I must have exhausted you, forgive me. I've been very happy. I hope I haven't achieved that by making you unhappy.' They murmured dissent and pleasure back to him gallantly; she thought they meant it. 'Tomorrow at eleven. And I promise not to work you so hard again.'

It wouldn't be necessary. If, of course, he took up that baton again tomorrow at eleven! That gained, they had time, plenty of time.

Lucas moved down purposefully among his team, exchanging a word here, a word there, to be remembered, perhaps, to be recorded. Or perhaps only to encourage them, if he did not come back, to look at the work he had rehearsed with them, and somehow give it the positive form which alone could deliver it to the world. Encountering Mike Brace, as that young man edged his way determinedly out of the press, he said with a sudden flashing smile: 'Very nice performance, Mr Brace. I should cut out running, if I were you, it's even worse for the wind than cigarettes – especially before rehearsals.'

He passed on without waiting for an answer. Mike, with a kindling eye, wormed his way clear of the wind section, and looked round for Una. She saw him coming, and slipped through one of the glass doors into the silence of the deserted corridor beyond. He came shouldering his way through after her, and reached for her hand. He had left the precious horn behind him, unguarded in the hall; that was a measure of his urgency. And he was a funny and endearing sight, flushed pink with his exertions under that wild yellow hair. Dead serious, and so sharply focused on something he could see, but she couldn't, that her heart rose in a wild surge of faith and hope.

'Una, listen! I've got to go out of Gries. Not far, I'll be back this evening. Watch out for me on the island, will you? Even if it's late. I don't know how long it's going to take me. But I'll come. I will come!'

'Mike, have you found out something? Are you on to something? Really?'

Lucas wouldn't be long. Just five minutes of touching and leaving impressions with his hands and his mind. And she didn't want him to know anything about what Mike Brace was doing, not yet. Whatever it was! She didn't know, and there was hardly time to ask; she had simply to believe.

'I think I'm on to something – I *think* so! I'm playing a hunch, and I don't *know* that it's going to come off. I just don't know. But if it does fit . . . Let's give it a chance, eh? And don't fret, even if this falls down on us. I'll think of something else.'

'I believe you, Mike,' she said. Who would have

thought they had met only yesterday, and in such crazy circumstances? Though maybe this was crazy, too, in its own way, this headlong encounter. It felt reasonable enough to her, secure as the ground she walked on. 'I believe you will. And it isn't even your worry! I'm ashamed to let you lift it from me, but you *do*!'

'Good! Stick to that!' He sounded suddenly a little drunk, but not with alcohol, or with music, either. 'Would there be any other little thing I could relieve you of?'

There was, and he took that, too. No one else appeared in the corridor. Or, momentarily, the world.

'I suppose,' she said, emerging dazedly, 'you're one of those people who could be described as having taking ways.'

'And what are you? A cheerful giver?' He kissed her again, very quickly and shyly and kindly, not fooling any longer, not even pretending to be cheeky about it. 'I've got to borrow a motor-bike.'

'Mike – don't you need money? To hire one?'

'No, it's all right, I've got a friend – up on the fairground.'

This time it was he who turned back at the last moment to offer her an impulsive gift. 'You know what? Your old man's all right! Even just on my own account, now, let alone yours, I wouldn't allow anything to happen to him.'

CHAPTER TEN

She had not asked anything, or doubted anything. It would have been like trying to halt a hurricane, and one that was on her side. When he was gone she waited a little while, standing alone in the white corridor behind the hall, a little numbed with the unexpectedness of it. She had never felt so sure of anyone, or so independent of all others, until now.

When she slipped back through the glass door, Lucas was already working his way by instinct towards the exit, and looking round for her. She went to his side, composing her face into the daughterly shape required of her, though she no longer felt like a daughter, or certainly not to the exclusion of other and more disturbing identities. They reached the outer door together, and passed through it into the sunlit courtyard.

They looked at each other along braced shoulders, like friends, not like father and daughter. She had never felt more tender and fond towards him, perhaps because he had just surrendered something, and did not yet realise it. He looked exhausted but relaxed, as though he had just gained something, too, and had not yet had time to assess it.

'Good?' she said.

'Good. Better than I expected. That boy will be a great horn-player, among the greatest. In five years, perhaps, or six, the world will know about him. I don't have to tell him, he knows it. Or to warn him, either, he knows the odds against, and the dangers of over-confidence. I'm glad to have heard him,' he said, withdrawing into his private place, 'though he was not at his best today, I should guess. Fractured. I wonder why?'

The big black car was waiting in the shadow across the courtyard. Crista got out of it, and came to meet them.

'If you don't mind, Mr Corinth, Herr Wehrle is here in Herr Graf's office, and would like you to look in before you leave.'

'Of course,' said Lucas resignedly, withdrawing his mind from music with the lingering implication of pain; and they followed her along more corridors to a quiet rear room where Wehrle waited for them.

It was Heinz-Otto Graf who sat squarely behind the big desk, with the light from the window on his left hand; but it was Dieter Wehrle who dominated the conference that followed, without asserting himself, without doing the lion's share of the talking, without even raising his voice. As usual, he had no attendant officer at his elbow to take notes, and took none himself, but clearly he knew everything that had happened at the Himmelhof since Lucas's banishment to that delectable prison. Nor would he forget a word of what was said now.

'I had thought,' he said, when they had been over every circumstance, 'of having a boat patrol tonight. But apart from being short of men and exciting too much attention from people in the town, I decided against it. It might escape the notice of the public, with care, it certainly could not escape the notice of a person bent on the kind of attack we are trying to prevent. We should succeed only in postponing it. He would be warned off at once, and lie in ambush for a better opportunity. And we should be no nearer finding him. I prefer to rely on the same precautions we have adopted so far. And perhaps one added one.'

'We've had a surfeit of warnings,' Lucas said in a resolutely matter-of-fact voice, 'but so far nothing has happened. I begin to believe that nothing will happen – that you might just as well withdraw your guard altogether from the island. I'd go so far as to bet that we're in for a perfectly quiet night.'

'I cannot be sure of that,' said Wehrle simply.

Lucas didn't believe it, either. He had been careful not to say what he actually meant, because Una would not have liked it any better than Wehrle. What was really in his mind was that whatever was going to happen had better happen soon. Neither side could stand this strain for long. If the police could be induced to go away, perhaps Valentine would materialise at last. He was beginning to look forward to that encounter as the only way out of the impasse, the only means by which he could ever discover the true extent of his guilt, or hope for peace for himself or that poor boy. There were times now when he felt closer to Valentine Gelder than to anyone in the world, even Una. His daughter was at his side, watching over him with absolute loyalty; but Valentine's son was inside him, dissolved into his flesh and spirit. What kind of childhood, what kind of adolescence, had the boy had, if now at the end of it he was poised and dedicated thus entirely to a single hate?

Lucas, who had loved and pitied himself as tenderly as most men, was being reorientated to love and pity of the enemy who threatened him, and whose case was gradually coming to seem to him so much more tragic than his own.

'I am still responsible for protecting you,' said Wehrle, 'and I don't intend to leave anything to chance. Before tonight I hope to have a further report on Frau Gelder's movements after she left here. Meantime, I'm afraid you will have to reconcile yourself to being nursed. But at least it seems we can be easy about this young Englishman of yours. There is one more thing we can do.'

He opened the drawer in the right-hand corner of Herr Graf's massive desk, and laid upon the leather-faced top between them a small black gun.

'For you, Mr Corinth. As an additional precaution.'

Lucas recoiled visibly, shaking his head. 'No, thank you. I don't carry a gun.'

'You have done so, I think, on occasion. You were accustomed to them once, no doubt you're still competent to handle them with responsibility.'

Yes, Lucas had handled them in his time. Just such a pistol as this he had carried more than once on those mountain journeys, and been prepared to use at need. Had used, at least once. He sat staring at the little, inert thing lying there innocently on the desk. An Austrian-made Steyr .32, to a design originally brought out by the Belgian Pieper gunsmiths. Nearly seven inches long, weighing nearly a pound and a half, and able to put a bullet through from four to five inches of pine board at fifteen to twenty feet. Rather an uncomfortable and unwieldy thing to carry undetected in a well-fitting suit. Even smaller calibre guns can kill, at close quarters. This one was meant to be a killer.

'I won't carry fire-arms. I appreciate the offer, but I can't accept it.'

'Why not? You can't afford to take any risks,' urged Graf, thinking of his investment.

No, Lucas couldn't afford to take any risks with Valentine Gelder's life. That was precisely the reason why he could not go armed.

'I have a revulsion against them now,' he said, frowning. 'I have every confidence in your ability to protect me, if you insist on my retaining the guard. But don't ask me to use fire-arms myself.'

He heard the rustle of a skirt behind him, and a hand touched his arm in urgent appeal. He looked round, expecting Una's reproachful face, and looked into the dark eyes of Crista Lohr.

'Please!' she said quietly. 'Take it!'

The hand at his sleeve was trembling slightly, he felt its vibration in his own flesh. Did it matter so much to her? And why? For his sake, or because she felt herself to be carrying the honour of the town in her hands, and would take it to heart as a personal failure if she let anything happen to him? She was an advanced case of conscience and professional pride, but there might be a grain of awareness of Lucas as a person, too, mightn't there? It was she who had touched him this time.

'I'm sorry, Crista, but I can't.'

'Please!' she repeated, hardly above a whisper. 'I should be so much happier.'

'But I shouldn't,' he said firmly. 'No, that's one thing you mustn't ask of me.' He looked up at Wehrle, and from the corner of his eye he saw Herr Graf heave up his massive shoulders in a fatalistic shrug. 'Put it away. I haven't touched a gun since I got to England. I don't want to renew that acquaintance now.'

Wehrle knew determination – or obstinacy? – when he saw it confronting him. Without argument he opened the drawer and slipped the Steyr back into it. The very heft of it in his grasp conveyed to Lucas that it was loaded. He remembered the balance of such a pistol in his hand, and the slight drag of its weight in his pocket on the way up the Filsertal in the dark, many a time.

'As you please. We shall do our best to make it irrelevant in any case.'

The car was waiting in the courtyard. Lucas went out to it empty-handed, as he had preferred, and was ferried back to his island in the early evening's radiant calm, in a placidity and silence which had much of resignation in them, but little of peace.

'Don't blame me,' he said suddenly, in the car. 'It isn't that I won't do everything possible to keep my life. But that isn't the way.'

'No,' said Una, no less quietly. 'I understand that. I'm with you.'

He had not fully realised, until she answered him, that it was to Crista he had been speaking.

*   *   *

It was a golden twilight. Even after the sun had dropped behind the peaks of the Silvretta, the after-glow lingered in a dazzling sky for longer than usual, and cast an opalescent reflection over the surface of the lake, so that light seemed to be emanating from twin bowls of crystal, one above them and one below. The tips of the mountains deepened to a dusky blue in contrast to the brightness behind them. From the windows on the sheer side of the island they could see the town still bathed in slanting sunlight, and every little motor-boat trail was a silver pencil-mark across the mirror of lilac water.

They had eaten the dinner the two girls had cooked in partnership, and drunk their coffee, lingering over it. They had washed up and put away the antique china plates and the modern cooking pots that matched so oddly. Geestler was making his evening round of the whole cascade of gardens and pavilions. Richard Schwalbe patrolled close to the house. In only a little over twenty-four hours, this had become normality. And yet Una's unease grew with every moment.

It distilled from Lucas. His calm was unnatural and frightening to her. What was the use of Mike Brace scouring the Tyrol on his borrowed motor-bike in search of a possibly unfindable witness, if Lu sat here communing with his own secret mind, and more and more surely reconciling himself to being a sacrifice? Almost as if he did not really want his old friend's son – his own enemy – to fail of what he had set out to do.

True, he neither did nor said anything now to suggest that he was even aware of a death hovering over him. He talked sensibly, he ate well, he was – what should one call it? Relaxed? Apathetic? Hypnotised? – at any rate, coherent and equable, with none of the momentary acidities or flares of impatience that were common with him. Considerate with her and with

Crista to the point where it began to seem almost unnatural. Rather as though the waiting death had drawn so close to him now that he could not see it, because it was out of focus, though in the core of his mind he knew where it was, and was unconsciously waiting for the hand to be laid on his shoulder.

Una was leaning with Crista on the crumbling wall of the terrace, their backs turned to the window of the salon, which was not yet lit. Lucas was at the harpsichord, playing from memory morsels of Bach and Mozart and Couperin, playing with complete control and total absorption. Una had a macabre vision of one more in the long mediaeval cycles of the 'Dance of Death', a panel none of the artists had ever painted: The harpsichord-player. The man sitting rapt at the keyboard, wholly concentrated on the score before him, and the long, bony hand reaching over his shoulder to turn the page for him.

'If only,' she said, 'there was something we could do!'

'They've done everything,' said Crista, 'everything one can think of.'

'Have they, though? They've covered all the obvious approaches, I know, and they'll be on watch all night, between the two of them. All this face of the house is checked, all the doors and windows – I know. But the place sprawls over so much ground, and there are so many ground-floor windows.'

'They go round them all and shutter them, after dark.'

'Yes, but even the other side, the cliff side . . . I don't believe all the shutters are closed – or else some of them have dropped from their hinges. Don't you remember how the light reflected from glass, when we were looking up from the boat?'

Now she recalled clearly one or two winking stars, high above the rocks. Rocks so broken that here and there, for all the entire townward face appeared sheer, there might be places where it could be climbed.

'We could check them, if you like,' suggested Crista. 'It would be better than doing nothing. We could cover all the other side of the house, see that the windows are fastened, close the shutters, if they're open – lock the doors of the rooms if there are any where the shutters are broken.'

'A good idea! We can soon do it between us. Start from the central block, and then work outwards both ways along the wings.'

She had revived at the prospect of having some activity, at least potentially useful, to occupy her hands and her mind. It might be closing only a few insignificant chinks in their armour, but it was something. And from every window, as she went from room to room, she would be watching for the silver pencil-mark that did not curve and return to the town, but sheered straight ahead for the southern point of their island and the landing-stage beyond. He had said he would come, however late, and she had acquired, in one day, a great deal of confidence in Mike Brace.

'We should tell him,' said Crista.

'Him?' Una was momentarily lost.

'Otherwise he may miss us and wonder where we are. He might come looking for you. Better he should stay here,' Crista said.

'Yes, you're right. I'll tell him.'

She went into the salon, and suddenly the back view of Lucas at the keyboard stopped her in the doorway, and held her still for a moment, watching him. His spine was long and slender and very straight, the neck and head set elegantly back to continue the erect line. The back of his head was beautiful and young. He had the intense fragility that is made to last, apparently, for ever, every line fine-drawn, with an edge like steel; and suddenly she wondered if Crista would have seen him in the same terms, if she had done this errand instead, and what would have replaced for her the spurt of maternal tenderness which had halted Una in her tracks.

He finished a Mozart minuet, played with the keys absently for a moment; and then he felt her there, and turned and smiled.

'Lu, Crista and I are going round all the ground-floor rooms over the lake, to make sure everything's secured.' She went close to him, and laid a hand experimentally on his shoulder. If death dared do that, why shouldn't life, too? It might even act as a charm against evil. 'We won't be long. Go on playing. We shall hear you, every time we come back to the colonnade.'

'What would you like?' he asked, picking out single notes for their brief sweetness while he waited for her orders.

'Biber's "Battle" – all of it.' It was long and complex and staggeringly original and modern, considering it was nearly three hundred years old, and it had been one of her favourites ever since she had learned to take delight in the more modest harpsichord Lu had acquired at a county auction sale. It had more movements than she could remember, and it should keep him busy, and with at least the illusion of an audience, until she came back to him. 'Don't forget the drum effects, will you?'

'I won't,' he promised. And by the time she had reached the doorway he had squared his shoulders and flexed his memory, and was launched on the first movement of *La Battalia*.

Crista walked with her round the colonnade to the main block of the house, with head erect and ears pricked, almost reluctant to withdraw from that lovely, lively, spirited sound.

'He plays so beautifully,' she said, grieving.

'Yes. I'm not sure,' said Una with arrogant honesty, 'that he's a genius, but I do know he doesn't fall far short. He likes to think of himself as a composer. And second as a conductor. But I've known him best as a performer, and that's how I think of him.'

'He gives concerts, too? At home?'

'Not often, but very occasionally he does. He likes conducting better. He plays the oboe, too. Well, he can play most things, if he puts his mind to it. It's his language, you see. Once you know the classic tongue, it's only like catching up with the dialects.'

They had reached the end of the curving wing, where the colonnade brought them to a small door that led into the main block. Within, a corridor pierced directly through, bisecting the main hall beneath the great staircase, baroque and dual, its twin arms encircling a statuary group of Venus in her dove-drawn car.

'Do we look upstairs, too? You think we ought to?'

The empty corridors, arched and encrusted with heavy decorative plaster, rang hollowly to the clicking heels of their sandals. All those dilapidated splendours, the pale blue and gold satins dropping into holes on the chairs and couches, the damask-panelled walls, the crazy, uncomfortable Empire furniture, the elaborate white ceramic stoves crowned with bulging vases and coy nymphs, the ceilings encrusted with chipped *putti*, all smelled of the past, a cool, damp, faintly spicy smell, as remote from danger as the fierce, heartening smell of breakfast coffee. Effete ghosts might creep in here, but not armed enemies. Even the ghosts would be as flimsy as the china flowers growing in broken profusion round the frames of the mirrors, incapable of harm.

They parted on the upper landing, Una going to the right, Crista to the left, and passed from room to room, testing the catches of the windows, drawing the creaking shutters to and fastening them with the iron peg that bolted them close. Room after room darkened on their heels. As yet there was no power connected here, only in the living quarters. Again they met on the landing above the staircase, and descended together into the hall.

'Toss you,' said Una, fishing a forgotten five-schilling piece out of the pocket of her skirt, 'who goes which way.'

'No, you began that way, let's go on like that.' It would bring Una back gradually to the inhabited part, and to Lucas, while Crista laboured longer in the deserted wing. She understood, even before Crista continued, almost deprecatingly: 'You should go back to him first. It will be better.'

'All right! Yes, I'll go.'

In the direct path of Venus's chariot they separated, Crista going on by the ground-floor rooms on the distant side, and so round into the damp and decaying glories of the forsaken wing, Una turning back to comb the lower storey on her own side, and work her way back to Lucas. For a time they heard each other's tiny, lonely foot-falls clashing on the tessellated floors and marble corridors, and vanishing into mouldering carpets and the muffling quietness of dust-sheets and heavy curtains. Then each of them was alone, the only source of sound in all that majestic silence.

Everything was changed for Una from that moment. She imagined echoes of her own footsteps, following somewhere a few paces behind; but when she turned her head there was no one to be seen. She saw brocade curtains swing as though a hand had just let them fall, and the gimcrack tinsel and gilt of the panelling, as she opened the door of room after room, seemed to tremble with a reflected presence just flashing out of sight. She went methodically through the ground-floor rooms of her side of the main block, testing window catches, clamping shutters together where they were not already closed. Occasionally, when she came near to the hall again, she heard Crista's sandals clicking in time with her own, somewhere there on the opposite side. But more and more distantly, as they drew apart. Crista was moving more briskly than she, perhaps aware of having farther to go. After they lost touch with each other, new and strange sounds moved in and took possession of the silence, the mysterious, rustling sounds of all unused houses.

From every window she looked out toward Gries, to

see if the darkening water bore anywhere the darker speck of a boat; but now the pleasure cruisers had drawn in for the night, and there was no sign, only a great pewter stillness before the true, cobalt darkness fell. She came back, walking softly, to the rear part of the hall, her round completed. No, not completed! There was a narrow little door under the staircase, hidden behind Venus's billowing draperies. Of course, the passage to the lantern on the promontory must begin here, it was the centre-point of the view from the town. Had Crista checked the little chamber there? She thought not, for Crista was ahead of her, and had vanished into the recesses of the other wing.

She tried the little door, white, etched in curvilinear gold, and it gave to her hand. Was it possible for anyone to get in by way of that ostentatious little summer-house on the rock, and so enter the house? The cliff below it looked sheer, but she had seen it only from the water. Better make sure.

The passage was panelled all the way in the same white, soiled now with the dust of years, engraved with tarnished gilt. It was lit from above, and an astonishing amount of light still spilled into it, for half the panes of glass above were broken, and she trod over tinkling crystal shards as she walked. The floor was mosaic, cold through her thin soles, and with arms half-extended she could touch both walls.

She came to a second door like the first, and beyond was the small hexagonal room she might have expected, the three walls towards the water all windows, the other three painted with odiously coy nymphs and lewd Cupids, the arched ceiling ebullient with cloud-borne deities. Rococo always made her feel puritan in recoil, it ogled and leered so. She averted her eyes from the indecent pink balloons of flesh, still visible in the afterglow and the reflections from the water, flaking off in leprous patches, bulging where more flakes were about to fall, like some obscene skin disease, and went straight to the window, to peer out again towards the town. She felt like the lookout in Bluebeard. 'Sister Anne, Sister Anne, do you see anyone coming?'

She was scrubbing at the dusty glass with her handkerchief when the tiny, crisp, metallic sound at her back made her stiffen where she stood. For an instant she held her breath, ears pricked to listen more intently, then she whirled and flung herself across the paved floor to clutch the handle of the door in both hands, and twist and tug at it with all her strength, but it did not move. She laid her ear against the painted panels, and listened again, but she heard no sound of a footfall. Whoever had come had come silently, and as silently departed. The door was locked, and she was a prisoner.

CHAPTER ELEVEN

For fully two minutes she continued to wrestle with the door-handle, almost convinced that it had merely jammed, that she had not pressed it far enough to release the catch, though she knew in her own mind that the key had been turned. Arduously she span the handle to its limit, but the door remained immovable. Then, realising that she was out of range of anyone's hearing except, possibly, Crista's, and that with every moment of delay Crista must be moving briskly and dutifully away from her, leaving her utterly isolated, she cupped her hands round the great keyhole, and kneeled to turn them into a trumpet for her mouth, and shouted Crista's name time after time with all her might. When she listened, between shouts, trying to silence her heaving breath, no sound replied. Crista was already out of earshot, surely, more than half the bulk of the house between them. And besides, if there was an intruder already inside the Himmelhof with them, and Crista came running back to her, what might happen to Crista?

The door fitted closely into its jamb, but the large keyhole seemed to offer at least a possibility of being able to pick the lock. Her summer dress had a narrow belt with a long buckle, and therefore a long steel tongue. She unfastened it, and went to work with eyes half-closed, feeling her way into the interior of the lock with fierce concentration; but five long minutes of cautious wrestling left her with damp forehead, bruised and numbed fingers, and no sign of any yielding in the lock.

She scrambled up from her knees, and looked round for a better weapon, for she was sure the key had been removed from the lock on the other side. But there was nothing in the tower room but one draggled chair, and no latch or bar of metal on the windows that she could hope to detach and use. And even if there had been a tool handy, she doubted if she could move that massive lock via the keyhole.

Clearly she could shout until she was hoarse, and no one would hear her. Even if these rooms had been supplied with electric light, or she had carried a torch, any signals she flashed would surely have passed unregarded. Her windows faced the lake, she was detached from the main body of the house by the closed passage, and from all its inhabited parts by a considerably greater distance. If the design was to separate her from Lu, and prevent her from giving any warning of the approach of the enemy, she could not have been trapped in a more effective place.

She had often wondered how she would react in an emergency. Prior consideration on that score was obviously pointless, for in the end it all depended on what was at stake. If she had been in fear for herself, of starving to death here undiscovered like the bride in *The Mistletoe Bough*, she would probably have wasted time and energy in battering at the door, and screamed herself hoarse and desperate trying to fetch someone to her aid. But what mattered in this crisis was to get out of here and get to Lu's aid. Having tried her art on the door and her lungs on yelling, and found both inadequate, she stood stock-still in the middle of the floor, and thought deliberately, almost coldly, through the sparse possibilities.

Not the door, that was out. Except by some far-fetched accident she was unlikely to attract the attention of anyone in the house. A light was out of the question, so she had no means of signalling her plight to Gries or even to a boat. Mike had said he would come, however late, and Mike was a man of his word, but whoever had turned the key on her would not wait. There remained the window as a way out. Rock beneath, and surely deep water under it, but diving would be far too foolhardy. Well, at least she could look.

The two side windows were fixed, the central one was designed to open. She got the inner pane opened, and struggled with the rusty catch of the outer one, and when it defied her hands, being corroded into an inseparable block with its socket, she stepped back into the room and looked round for her only tool, the draggled satin chair. It stood against the wall on curving, slender legs, its mildewed stuffing dangling. She picked it up by its gilded back, with the seat as a shield before her face and her bare arms, and jabbed the carved legs viciously through the glass.

One leg of the chair, eaten with worm, crumbled away almost into powder, but the other three stabbed through the barrier with a sound like the parting of ice-floes on a spring river, and the whole great pane, its tension shattered, sprang outwards and rang in a shivering fall down the rocks. The thin, slithering echoes seemed to go on for a long time. She could hear them still drifting and tinkling when she had battered away the daggers of glass that clung in the edges of the window-frame, and carefully wedged the chair over the jagged fringe that remained, so that she could lean over and look down.

What had seemed a sheer drop did not look quite so precipitous from here, especially to the left side of the sharp little promontory. The lantern stood on a small, rough headland jutting like the prow of a ship, and terminating in a space three yards square, or a little more, of uneven but relatively level rock. She climbed carefully out over the sill, leaving the chair propped in place so that she could get back if she had to.

She saw at once that from this little eyrie there was no external way back to the rest of the house. She had hoped it might be possible to work her way along by the outside wall of the passage, and climb in again at one of the house windows, even if she had to break her way through some shutter she herself had just fastened from within. But the walls of the passage ran down flush into the rock on both sides. There was no way back except by water. The thought of risking a dive, even from the most favourable point, at this height, with inadequate knowledge of the shore below, made her stomach turn over. Far more likely to hit the rocks than the water. But if only she could climb down towards it, even part of the way, and get a better look at the hazards, it might be feasible. She wasn't afraid of the swim, she had been at home in water since she was three or four years old.

She edged forward to the brink of the descent, towards the left, where it looked least abrupt. There was an iron stanchion, as thick as her wrist, driven into the rock close to her feet, she kicked it before she was aware, and recoiled in sharp fear at the tremor it caused in her balance. It was dusk now, she had to peer cautiously at the broken formations of rock she trod, here where she felt herself assailed on every side by air that at once supported and tugged at her – like the figure-head of some stone ship. She went down on her knees to escape that frightening persuasion, and then stretched out flat on her face, looking down over the edge. The stanchion, jutting about nine inches from the rock, was comforting to cling to, for when she gripped it she found it solid and immovable as the cliff itself. From its round eye a frayed tassel of wire rope stood up several inches more, like an aigrette. She felt downwards from the eye in which it was secured, and found that the wire rope ran down as far as she could reach, over the rim and into the dusk of the rocks. She shook it experimentally, and it resisted the movement, no more than quivering in her grasp. Somewhere below it was secured again, just as firmly. And below that?

How would she ever know, unless she tested it? She

edged forward until head and shoulders hung over the void, and holding fast with her right hand, felt down along the surfaces of rock with the other.

Beneath the first near-vertical drop, no more than twelve or thirteen inches deep, the rock levelled again. What was more, her fingers felt it curiously smoothed, as though men had helped to shape it. A step! Begun by the natural formation, but finished off, surely, by man, just as man had driven in those stays and fixed that solid wire handrail. And if that was true, it ought not to terminate halfway, it must have been meant at some time to provide a workable way down to the lake, for those used to such short-cuts. Someone, at least, had used it, or it wouldn't be here. And where someone else had gone she could go. If she could get down to the water she could swim round to the beach, she wasn't afraid of that part.

She turned, clinging to the stanchion, and backed gingerly into the void, groping with one foot for the second step. It was there, cut and shaped, level enough to give her a good hold. She brought her other foot down to join the first, holding the rope with both hands, breathing now into the blue-black crevices of the rock. Without that handrail she would never have dared to venture like this. She wasn't afraid of heights, or of the voids they presented around them, provided there was a firm handhold to cling to. Descending even a vertical ladder is simple and easy while you have the firm round rungs to fill your hands; and this rock face, sheer and lofty though it was, was not quite vertical, and varied by many striations and crevices that afforded comforting footholds. But don't look down, she thought. That's the one fatal thing to do.

She had preferred not to think of the possibility that the wire rope might, after all, end halfway, having served its purpose for climbers more accomplished than herself; or that it might somewhere have broken loose from its moorings, or even parted and rusted away, for it must have been neglected for many years. But at every yard of progress she gripped and shook it again, and so far it held firm below her, giving no more than her balance could bear.

She was some ten yards down the cliff, braced and reaching down with stretched toes for the next foothold, when she heard the shot.

It was only a small, flat sound, away there on the other side of the dark hulk of the house, where the lighted windows were and the sheltered garden terraces. It should not, by rights, have reached her ears at all, but passed, muted, above her head; but it did not, it spat its dry crack into the pure, still air of the evening, and let it diffuse like a monstrously accelerated ripple across the face of sky and lake, everywhere carried and repeated, a scar across the silence.

She knew what it was, and her heart leapt sickeningly into her throat. She shut her eyes and hung shivering with nausea for a moment, thinking of Lu sitting at the harpsichord, comforted and charmed, absorbed into the astonishing devices of 'La Battalia', and of death reaching a bony hand over his shoulder to turn the page for him. And of Crista, turning from her devoted labours in the distant wing and running wildly along the echoing colonnade towards the sound, while she, who had the better right to love him, hung there spread-eagled like a fly in a spider's web, and couldn't even run to him.

She came out of that paralysis in an explosion of vigour and anger and resolve, gripping the rough wire and letting herself slide backwards, feeling with frantic toes for the next hold. The rusty strands tore her fingers, her sandals slipped on the irregular planes of stone, but the crude giant steps continued, and somehow she scrambled and slid and fell down them, divorced from fear. It felt like going away from him, but it was the only way back to him.

For a time she moved and thought and acted in a

misty and limited world of shock and rage, where concrete things like the rock against her breast, the lapping water below her, the crumbling rope that scorched her palms, were hardly real to her at all, and her mind, detached from her own extremity, grappled with vital realities. The police had guns, if Lu had refused the one offered to him. It had to be Geestler or Schwalbe who had fired. They wouldn't leave him, not both of them, one would be always on call. Some false alarm, a movement in the gardens, an animal rustling in the bushes . . . God, don't let it be anything more than that!

Sound carries well over water, she remembered, somewhere in a chill, logical chamber at the core of her furious mind. And she hung still for a moment, turning her head to shout across the plashing surface of the Himmelsee, now so close beneath her. There had been a boat abroad at night once, there might be again. She held her breath to listen for a reply. Nothing. Only the loose, watery sound of the lake lipping at the rocks, like a dog lapping at a bowl. Step by invisible step she groped backwards, and with every yard the air darkened and stilled about her, but she was so inured to the dusk by this time that she hardly noticed.

Once, feeling herself very near now, she anchored herself firmly, and deliberately turned and looked down. At the foot of the face of cliff the rocks spread out in a low ridge into the water; there was even a narrow level of hard soil, terminating in the rotting remains of a little wooden stage, long disused, half its planks trailing. From that she could get safely into the water.

She touched one foot to the last level, and shakily brought the other down to join it, and her knees quivered under her. Here there was room to stand, even to move; she was no more than six feet above the water. Gingerly she loosened her convulsive grip on the rope, and smoothed her scratched palms achingly down her thighs. Hugging the rock face, she felt her way along to the edge of the broken landing-stage.

There was flooring enough to stand on, a shaky rail, and a ladder down into the lake. It would do. She kicked off her sandals, hardly noticing when one of them slid over the edge and vanished in a minute phosphorescent fountain in the shallows. She was kneeling at the edge of the stage with her ruined dress half over her head when she heard the sound for which she had been waiting; and she was so far lost in her own solitary struggle that it had been throbbing distantly in her ears for half a minute before she realised what it was. It came so subtly and gradually out of nowhere, a low-pitched, busy, dotted-line of a sound, like a cat purring. Somewhere out there in the dark a motor-boat was shearing westward through the water, headed for the southern point of the island.

When she had tugged down her dress again, and reared her head to stare, she could see the faint, fine line of phosphorescence prolonging itself across the blue-black of the Himmelsee. It looked a long way off, it was crossing her field of vision steadily from left to right, unaware of her, abandoning her here if she did not do something quickly to assert herself.

She cupped her hands about her mouth, threw back her head, and hallooed again and again at the full stretch of her lungs, without even realising that she was crying Mike's name, calling him to her on fierce, commanding notes of appeal and possession, demanding that he hear and understand.

She stopped only because she was exhausted, drained of breath and for the moment of energy and purpose. She clung to the insecure rail above the water, and staring out into the darkness, saw the dotted line of lambent light hesitate, and heel, and come about, turning towards her. And after a moment she heard her answer uplifted thin and clear into the night, the distant, gallant clamour of Roland's horn.

CHAPTER TWELVE

Lucas was halfway through *La Battalia* when he sensed that there was someone standing behind him, quite still, listening. He did not stop playing. The miniature but tremendous excitement of the virtuoso display he was staging for no one, the vulnerable stream of memory, too, which once broken could not be restored without deformation, kept him constant. But his hands were in perfect command at the moment, he could release a thread of his consciousness for communication. Without turning his head he said:

'Come in, if you like it. Come in and listen. I don't mind an audience.'

How did he know that it was neither Una nor Crista standing there hesitating in the doorway? For one thing, neither of them would have had to hesitate. For another, he was sensitive to the very texture of Una's presence, he would always know when she was within touch of him. And Crista? It was beginning to be like that with Crista, too. She did everything possible to be anonymous, and she had only to move a hand, and he knew it, only to feel a slight, a pain, a regret, and he was responsive to it. The more she hid, the more he was aware of her. The more she confined herself severely to her secretarial duties, the more he saw her diffused and pervasive and in possession. And this was neither Una nor Crista.

Whoever it was had come nearer, accepting the invitation, and was soundlessly edging towards his right shoulder. Lucas was aware of pleasure, curiosity and delight, all contained, because the battle was not yet over, and a movement too sudden, an inch too far, might snap the thread and bring those sparkling keys jangling into disharmony and ruin.

'Sit down,' said Lucas to the shadow that loomed behind him. 'Why not? Listen in comfort, if you like it.'

The shadow crept from him, with considerate quietness, stepping lightly in the thick carpet, and found a seat by the wall, retired and in darkness. The whole salon was in near-darkness now, dusk came swooping when it came at last, spread wings obliterating the light; that was the gift of the mountains. Lucas needed no light to complete what he had begun, threading all those brief, vivid movements like beads on a string, without a break, only the rapid, expert knot between. The whole formidable suite took some twelve minutes to play. By the time he ended it, the two girls should be on their way back.

He did not miss them; in a sense they were present with him now. He had discovered the perfect secret of integrity, the total concentration on one immaculate task in hand, whatever happened afterwards. He had even an entranced audience; the shadow in the twilit room was sitting braced and still, only a vibration emanated from it, and that was of taut and charmed attention.

The battle passed, echoing into the distance, the lament over the casualties grieved and diminished, life recovered, took fresh bearings, and resumed its pilgrimage. The lovely old instrument – it was almost worth all the anguish, to have been brought to this encounter with it – stood trembling and palpitating like a female creature that has given birth. And gradually the vibrations ebbed out of it and let it rest in stillness and silence. Lucas turned, and looked at his companion. This one had stood at his back unchallenged, and had ample opportunity to cut off both the music and the performer, had he so wished; and he had not done it.

Lucas had expected Geestler, who was known to play most keyboard instruments, and to be fond of music. He saw the slimmer, more youthful outline of Richard Schwalbe, braced upright and alert, and with round young eyes fixed upon him.

'It's you, Richard? I didn't know you liked this kind of thing.'

'I didn't know, either,' said the dark swallow, and laughed. 'You didn't need light? No music? You weren't making that up?'

'No,' said Lucas, tired and sated, stroking the ivory keys that were like silk to the touch, 'I didn't make it up. I only wish I had but I merely arranged it. It was written by an amazing creature called Biber, in central Europe nearly three centuries ago. In Olomouc, in Moravia, I believe. For viols, originally. I know it by heart. I never played it better. I'm glad you were here to listen to it. I don't guarantee it was flawless, but I know I never made a better job of it. Will you remember I said that?'

'It sounded marvellous to me,' said Schwalbe joyously. 'I wanted to laugh and shout. Was that right?'

'That was right. Was that all?'

The boy pondered. 'One might also weep? Afterwards?'

'Many have,' said Lucas. 'I suspect this man Biber knew it, even while he was laughing and shouting. Richard, I enjoyed having you as an audience. Thank you! Will you have a drink?'

'No, no . . . I'm on duty, I must go. But thank you, all the same.' He was on his feet, backing deprecatingly towards the doorway, his smile gleaming in what remained of the light. 'I should be patrolling below.'

It was a strange thing, Lucas thought, turning back regretfully from the cabinet Heinz-Otto had stocked so generously with drinks, how everything that had given this young man his mystery and his perilous ambiguity in full daylight became crystal and understandable in the dark. His inscrutable gaiety, his brevity of speech, his distant enjoyment of the girls, that never made any attempt to draw nearer, all were human and touching and minor, instead of pagan and cool and incalculable. The dark swallow was encased in an impenetrable shell of shyness, and only music had drawn him through it for a moment. His purity was something no potential assassin, however motivated, could possibly afford. Valentine's passionate heat would have melted the shell long ago. This one was safe, simple and sweet, untouched by any corrosive hate, if he was not to be touched, as yet, by any disenchanting love. Some girl would lay her hand on his arm some day, and break the spell. But not, Lucas thought, either of my girls.

'Richard,' he said, before the boy reached the terrace and vanished, faun-like, into shadows, 'tell me something. When I lived here as a boy, I knew two families of Geestlers. Johann had a farm out beyond the castle. And there was a younger brother, Niklaus, with a smithy at the other side of the town. Which of them is your friend Hugo's father?'

It was hardly important, of course, since one of them must be. The age was right, and as far as he remembered, there were no more Geestlers here. Johann, the elder, possessor of the family farm, had been married already when Lucas left, and he thought there had already been one child, and another on the way. About Niklaus he had less clear memories. Hadn't he been courting a girl from one of the inns? Leni, who helped at the Sonne? Hard to distinguish those lost faces, after all this time, yet most of them must still be here, and not changed out of all knowledge.

'His father has the smithy,' said Schwalbe readily. 'At least, it is not quite like that, he is not really their son. Herr Niklaus and Frau Leni took him as their own, because they had no children.' He let fall his bombshell gently and serenely, clearly only with a precise regard for truth, and knowing that everyone in Gries knew, and his friend was in no way sensitive about the relationship. A sensible family, without vulnerable secrets.

'You mean,' said Lucas, after a brief, blank pause, 'he is adopted?'

'He came to work for them, from an orphanage. And they liked him so much they took him legally for their own.' The faun shrugged wide, slender shoulders, and lit the dusk with his incandescent smile.

'I see. It seems both he and his – family – have been lucky,' said Lucas. 'Perhaps they knew his own parents?'

Richard hoisted those eloquent shoulders again, lightly and easily, with a different implication: What does it matter? They are all happy with the arrangement! 'I have no idea, I never spoke of it with him.'

'No, of course not! It's of no importance. They have a good son, and he a good family. That's everything.' The boy hung in the doorway, patient and well disposed, and again shy, awaiting dismissal. 'Goodnight, Richard!'

'Goodnight, Herr Corinth!'

He was gone, as light of foot as a deer, across the terrace and down to his rendezvous midway of the approaches, where he should have been some ten minutes ago.

Lucas stood quite still until the light, descending echoes had danced away down the steps, not yet out of earshot but so withdrawn now that they seemed to belong among the remembered reverberations of drums, in the battle still vibrating somewhere in the air. So this, like everything he touched in his concern for his own life, turned and confronted him with a changed situation and an opponent still elusive. Geestler, the one who was so safe because he *was* a Geestler, turned out to be only one by adoption. And there was hardly time now, even if there had been opportunity, to entice him into the same intimacy that had just been established with his friend, and see through him as clearly, and know the truth.

Adopted, after he had come – by his own choice? Lucas knew very little of how boys in public care are placed in employment! – to work for a family in Gries. At what age, then? Fourteen or fifteen, certainly. After how many years in care? Who knew? But perhaps only a few, only the end of his childhood, after the seed of a lifetime's hate and an inescapable duty of revenge had been implanted too deeply ever to be erased. Yes, it could be so.

But then, why had he not acted already? He had been trusted implicitly (though God knows, Lucas thought, that might in itself be a powerful deterrent against action!) and had surely had opportunities enough. But had he? When Lucas came to think back over their association, how many real opportunities had there been? When had they been alone together? There were five people here, and no harm, surely, intended to the girls. And Valentine would not be so lost to the compulsion of his own youth as to write himself off by acting openly, in front of witnesses. He had the rest of his life to live, he had to preserve his secrecy.

Lucas switched on the small lamp that stood on the drinks cabinet, poured himself a modest brandy and soda, and went on thinking. About those five people. Only this evening had this curious feeling of solitude found its way in here. The five people had dwindled to three. We won't be long, Una had said. But they hadn't come back. The two who were to be spared as much as possible seemed to have been temporarily eliminated from the scene. And now Richard Schwalbe, late for his patrol, was hurrying away. How if the girls had been ambushed and shut in, somewhere in those deserted splendours at the other end of the colonnade? How if the field was being cleared, now, at this moment, for the final act?

There is a way, he said to himself, of finding out. I could, of course, take a torch and go and look for the girls, but why bring them back on to the stage if they have been considerately removed for a good reason? If he doesn't want anyone else involved in the final encounter, neither do I. Someone else might get hurt. I prefer not to risk that. And I'm tired – how tired I am! – of sitting and waiting.

He took his glass, and crossed to the great window that looked out across the court to the opposite wing, and commanded a view of the whole terrace, and at least two shallow levels of the shrubberies below. Deliberately he drew back the curtains from every inch of the glass, and reaching out his free hand when that was done, switched on all the lights in the room, even the great chandelier, and stood framed in silhouette for the night to see. If Valentine wants me, here I am, let him come to me.

There was only a faint glimmer of starlight now on the marble and stone of the court, and a dim, greenish afterglow along the edge of the western sky. He could see, under the shadow of the colonnade, opposite, the faint reflection of the white balustrade refracted in oblique gleams in the panes of the last window in the forsaken wing, the fellow to this window at which he stood. With his face close to the glass he could even see down into the overgrown bushes and plaster caprices below the end of the other wing. Somewhere down there, out of sight, he heard Schwalbe raise a pure, shrill whistle to locate his colleague. Without success, for the whistle came again after the lapse of a few seconds.

And instant and sharp at the end of the whistle, before the silence could settle again, the shot split the night.

He heard the impact like a tiny, ringing echo. Eighteen inches or so above his head the tall pane of glass starred but did not shatter, and in the centre of radiating cracks the bullet-hole sat round and dark like a spider in its web. A few infinitely fine particles floated glittering in the light of the chandelier. A speck of blood on the hand that held the glass marked his only wound. He brushed away the silver of glass that had pricked him, and for several seconds he was not fully conscious that he had missed death by inches. The brandy in the glass was quite steady as he put it down on a table beside the window.

It was a great shout from Schwalbe, below in the garden, that brought him back to life. He sprang to the door, and out into the dimness of the colonnade, and ran to lean over the balustrade and peer below. Two terraces beneath him Schwalbe was running towards the great thickets of false acacia that shrouded the marble railings under the distant wing of the house. All the night was full of their drowning fragrance, as though they had been shaken and disturbed by a sudden wind, or the crashing flight of a fugitive. And indeed someone was already in among them, the bushes threshed and shook. From somewhere there, surely, the shot had been fired, and only the angle had caused it to miss him by so much. Not easy, from there, to shoot high enough to clear the balustrade, and still put the bullet through the window. Valentine had not done so badly. A mistake, though, to have attempted it from there.

Schwalbe saw him leaning over the railing, and checked for an instant in his headlong run to shout up at him: 'Go back! Go inside!'

Lucas had been about to launch himself down the steps in support, but he pulled up and swung round abruptly when Schwalbe insisted furiously: 'Go in! Take the girl inside and lock the door. Draw the curtains and stay inside!'

Lucas had not heard the steps behind him until then, light, frantic steps running towards him round the paved semicircle of the colonnade. He turned, hesitating, saw Crista's yellow dress glimmering in the darkness, and went in haste and concern to meet her, letting Schwalbe plunge on alone into the threshing bushes.

'It's all right, Crista, it's all right!' He took her by the shoulders, folded his arm round her, and drew her towards the blazing lights of the salon. Thank God she was intact, only frightened and shocked. She had heard the shot, and come rushing from whatever room she had reached in her tour of the dilapidated wing opposite. How like her, at any alarm to run towards him, not away! 'It's all right, you see I'm not touched.' He paused in the doorway to switch off the chandelier. 'Come along in, and I'll get you a drink. We could both use one.'

He stood back for her to enter the room before him, and then, passing her with a gentle touch on her arm to urge her towards a chair, he crossed to the window and drew all the curtains close before going to the cabinet and reaching into it for a second glass. She still had not uttered a sound, and the arm he had touched had felt like marble in his hand, cold with shock. It astonished him when he heard her move a few steps and turn the key in the lock. He smiled. She had always that intense sense of duty, she was taking no chances with him now.

'You'll have to open that again, you know,' he said reasonably. 'I've got to find Una before we raise the drawbridge and drop the portcullis. Where did you leave her?'

He turned with the glass in his hand, and looked into the round black eye of a small pistol.

His first thought was that she had privately accepted from Wehrle the protection he had refused, intent upon not failing in her charge. He even began to say, smiling: 'You're not going to need that . . .' But there he broke off. He had once known guns, Austrian-made guns at any rate, very well, and this was a smaller calibre thing, a good two inches shorter overall, with a stubby barrel and a wide, flat butt. He still knew the difference between a Steyr .32 and a little .25 Owa at sight. This one wouldn't put a slug through five inches of pine board at fifteen feet, but it would put one through a man, at pointblank range. And he had been wrong: she was going to need it. It was another charge she was intent on fulfilling, at all costs.

She had not moved. She stood with her shoulders braced back against the door, her great eyes fixed unwaveringly upon him. All the colour had drained from her face, and left her pale as marble, and stonily calm. The fine, competent hand was quite steady upon the butt of the gun. She held it as if it had been her familiar all her life, and could be relied upon absolutely to do her will now. He thought he had never seen anyone look so desperately sad.

So now he knew everything. He had what he had wanted; he was face to face with his enemy, and no policeman between them.

'I see!' he said in a long sigh, and the smile that had died on his lips came slowly back to them. 'You know, I've often read that a whisper has no character or sex or age, but one forgets to keep that kind of knowledge in mind. The one thing that never occurred to me was that the child might have been a girl! Now what am I to call you, Crista or Valentine?' She didn't answer, she seemed not to hear him; and no doubt both those names were hers. 'What have you done with Una?' She didn't answer that, either, but it didn't matter. She wouldn't hurt Una, her score was against no one but him. And the imaginary gunman in the garden, it seemed, need cause him no anxiety on anyone's account; he had already served his purpose.

'I wish you had accepted the gun,' she said, in a voice unnaturally quiet and dulled. 'It isn't going to be easy to kill you in cold blood.'

She had been consistent throughout, that fantastic touch of chivalry identified her beyond any doubt.

'Yes,' he said aloud, the faint smile warming into something very close to tenderness, 'you *are* his daughter, I see that. It wasn't my intention to make things harder for you, but I couldn't risk carrying a weapon. I never really got used to guns, you know. I might easily have done something I never meant to do.'

He reached behind him, and set down the glass very carefully. It would be a pity if it broke when he fell, it was Venetian, and old. To say nothing of the stain on the carpet – though, of course, the brandy wouldn't be the only stain.

'I suppose it was you who lobbed a stone into the bushes to draw Geestler away? And then shot out my window from the window opposite. Why didn't you shoot to kill then? I'm sure you could have. It would have been the easiest way.'

True, she was somewhat under-gunned for that distance, but he knew that was not the reason. She could have taken her stand somewhere closer if she had wished.

'I owed it to myself and you,' she said in the same soft, hopeless, relentless tone, not denying her ability, 'to face you as I killed you.'

'I'm grateful for that,' he said. 'I prefer it this way, too. To know you, and to have everything open and clear between us, that makes everything better. For me, and I hope for you. Now I have time to see death coming, as he did, and to understand how much I regret and resent it, and yet how little afraid of it I am when it comes to the point. And to realise that I bear you no grudge at all. Don't be afraid that I shall upset you by pleading for my life. That's no longer the main issue between us two.'

It was true. How and when had it happened, this metamorphosis, this release from the fear of fear and from all restraints? With almost no time left at all, no room for anything but absolute sincerity, all the non-essentials fell off like a cast skin. He looked her full in the face, gravely and gently, and said what he had to say.

'I'm more concerned for you. When you come round to believing my story, some day – as you will – remember that I said to you, you need never reproach yourself. I've always understood your position. Now I'm even becoming reconciled to my own. Yes, I was afraid, that night when I ran for the border. I was afraid when I waited over there in the woods. Yes, I was to blame. If I had stayed I might have died, too, but I might have been able to save him. It's not for nothing that I've had this burden on my mind all these years. Now it no longer distresses me. I behaved like a man, not a demi-god, because a man is all I am. So be it, I accept myself as I am, fallible, irresolute, complex, no hero. But I did my best with the material I had, and that's enough for me. I came to the meeting-place. Late, and shaking in my shoes, but I came.'

She said: 'I do not believe you.'

But how could she shut her mind against belief, she who had grown to know every wincing impulse that moved him, all his self-doubt and self-harrowing? He saw and was sorry for the suffering he had cost her since she had come to know him. All her dispositions for his privacy and protection, part of her rôle at first, had generated their own warmth as the hours passed, and become real, until now her whole instinct towards him was to guard and shield him, she who had all her life been waiting to fulfil herself by killing him.

'You needn't take my life,' he said gently, 'I give it to you, if that will make it better for you. All you have to do is squeeze the trigger, and remember afterwards that you did me no wrong. All you are doing is accepting a free gift from me. It's not much to give you, in return for what you've given back to me, my peace of mind.'

Her eyes seemed to grow still larger in her fixed and tormented face. She drew back her head against the door as though in recoil from a convulsion. He saw the corners of her lips contract. But she never stopped watching him, and her hand never wavered.

'You know how to turn everything to your advantage,' she said in a whisper, 'but it won't save you. I'm expendable, like you. What happens to me afterwards doesn't matter.'

'It matters to me,' he said. 'It's the only problem left. For God's sake, if there was no escaping this, why couldn't you put a second bullet in me out there on the terrace, and then throw the gun in the lake? Who would ever have thought of you? Now it's too late for that. There's got to be another way of saving you.'

She stepped away from the door, one long, steady pace, and slowly lifted the hand that held the gun, levelling it at his heart.

'I don't want to be saved,' she said. 'There will be nothing to survive for, why should I make the effort?'

He never knew why his heart turned in him at that, as though it had read into her despair something that had reversed suddenly into hope. Time was so short now that his thinking was done with his blood and his flesh, and the mind had no conscious part in it. Perhaps she had meant only that her life had been trained all into one narrow purpose, and once that was accomplished would have no further meaning. But perhaps that was not all, not the only source of the total emptiness of grief and desolation that he saw in her eyes. The world without her enemy was not worth the effort to keep it . . . or the world without Lucas Corinth, whatever he was, enemy or . . . ?

'Then it's up to me, isn't it,' he said, his eyes holding hers, 'to make the effort for you. I told you you could have my life, did I ever say you could have and throw away your own? I'll fight you for that as long as I have breath. I'll repeat and repeat to you that I have never told you anything but truth, and truth is what I'm telling you now, and you *shall* hear me, whether you want to or not, whether you kill me or not. Your father was my friend, the man I admired more than anyone I'd ever known, and the orders he gave me I carried out, to the letter, until there was a cordon between him and me, and I couldn't get to him. Yes, I was young, yes, I was afraid, yes, I would even have liked to run, but I did not. As soon as I could I came to the gate . . .'

'You're lying,' she said. 'Do you think I haven't heard this story a thousand times over from my mother? *They told her!* That you ran, with the papers that should have been for him—'

'*They told her! THEY?* The authorities? The Nazis who killed him? *She* might be crazy with her loss, and believe their word rather than mine, but can *you*? *She* might need a scapegoat, to make survival bearable, but do *you* need one?'

He watched her, and it seemed to him that somewhere in her deathly coldness some core of live, unsuspected heat had burned up suddenly, for two crimson flashes sprang into her icy cheeks, and two more into the blackness of her dilated eyes. It seemed, too, that there was a tremor from somewhere outside them both, that caused strange vibrations to flicker through the air, errant whispers like distant voices. If he could have detached enough attention to identify them they might even have been significant; but there was no longer anything of significance except the two of them, and the death condensing now very slowly in the crook of her forefinger.

'If you throw both our lives away now,' he said, 'at least I'll make sure you live the rest of yours, minutes or years, knowing that *they* lied, and *she* was mistaken, and *I* told you the truth you wouldn't hear.'

He had raised his voice, though he did not realise it, he was discharging the words at her with deliberate ferocity, like bullets.

'I did come. I did see a man standing in the darkness among the trees, I did call him by your father's name – *your* name.' He was watching her finger tighten, and the tension of waiting for the shot sharpened his utterance almost into a cry: 'I called out to him: *Valentine, Gott sei Dank*!'

The world rushed abruptly back in upon them like the recoil of a wave, bursting the bubble of their isolation, snatching away the last of his words, startling her into the first long tremor of feeling and horror. Yet she understood before he did. Outside the door a great, hoarse voice, a beery voice that might have well been dragged unwillingly out of an inn, was shouting in triumph that those were the words, that was the voice, that in all his life there had been only one such night, and how could he forget, in twenty-eight years or fifty, that encounter at the Filsertal gate?

And again and again the voice repeated, for vindicating emphasis:

' "*Valentine, Gott sei dank! – Gott sei dank! . . .*" '

And then hands rattled at the door-handle, and the anxious knocking began, and all the invading, clamouring voices demanding to be let in.

CHAPTER THIRTEEN

Lucas put up both hands to clutch at his head in a momentary access of faintness. The room went round. For an instant he even thought this might be dying, and he had somehow failed to feel the small puncture that was draining away the world from him like a stream of blood. Then his head cleared again, and sound and vision reassembled. She stood as before, motionless between him and the door, her face so drawn and exhausted that she might have been the one who had all but died.

The hand that held the gun had sunk to her side, and hung nervelessly. She did not seem able to move, or to turn away her eyes from his face. And outside the door a commanding fist was thumping for admittance, and the voices went on with their frightened threnody, Una's voice pleading with Lucas to be alive, and a young man's voice loudly urging that the door should be opened. It took Lucas a moment to identify his horn-player. Never before had he heard him sound so desperately in earnest.

The other voice was still there, too, it had been no illusion; that rough, chesty voice rumbling harshly in the depths, in broad local dialect, reiterating insistently: 'Those very words he cried to me that night – who else should know them? And I told him: They've taken him, I said, and they're looking for another – they're looking for you!'

She heard everything, and understood everything. Now there was no more power in her to move, or think or speak; she stood in a pale, exhausted stupor,

waiting for something, anything, to fill the vacuum
where the hate and the dedicated purpose had been. In
a sense she had died.

'Unlock the door,' shouted Mike Brace, shaking it
with the weight of his shoulder. 'We've found our
witness, he's here, he's ready to testify. You heard
him. Open the door!'

'I'm coming,' said Lucas mildly. 'Everything's all
right. Stop that noise!'

It stopped on the instant, on dead silence; and then
he clearly heard the long, soft, indrawn breaths, the
vast releasing sighs of relief and astonishment.

'Nothing whatever has happened,' he said firmly.
'I'll be with you in a moment.'

He went towards her, and she still seemed not to
hear or see him. But when he held out his hand
silently, she gave him the gun. He slipped it into his
pocket, and then, laying his arm gently about her
shoulders, drew her to a deep chair and put her into it,
turning it so that the high back sheltered her from the
sight of anyone entering the room.

Only then did he let them in. Una, soiled, crumpled
and barefoot, weak with reaction, but intact; her eyes
wide with mystification and – yes! – mistrust, her
hands scratched. Mike Brace breathless and bright-
eyed and uneasy, still clutching his horn in its shabby
case – did the boy take it to bed with him? And the
third, a lean dark bandit of a man under a limp old felt
hat, who slid his foot across the threshold as though
feeling for a possible step, and faced into the light
with unwinking eyes, turning his head sidelong from
one to another as they moved or spoke, with a sharp,
listening attention which made it clear that his ears
made up to him for another sense he lacked. And this
visitor, too, to add to the dreamlike surrealism of this
reunion, clutched a battered violin-case under his left
arm. The witness had known what he was about when
he had identified his man unseen. Lucas had talked in
the dark with a blind man.

'I'm all right,' said Lucas, briefly hugging Una to his heart, and even raising a concerned hand to stroke back her dishevelled hair and touch a long scratch on her cheek. 'Everything's all right now, nothing to worry about any more. It's I who should be worrying about you. Look at you! What have you been doing, climbing trees?'

'I'm all right – all I need is a bath and a clean dress. I . . . Lu, we thought – we heard the shot . . .' She looked over his shoulder to the arm of Crista's chair, and the pale hand that lay lax on the brocaded upholstery; and she looked into his face, and knew that he wanted her not to say anything of what she knew or guessed. He was alive and unhurt, and he had said that there was nothing to worry about any more. But there was more to it than that, something he had recovered, something that made him more complete than he had been before. She kissed him briefly and lightly instead of finishing the sentence. Whatever he wanted he should have; there would be a good reason for it. He was back in unmistakable command, and she was content with that.

'Mike's been all day looking for Herr Spindler,' she said, 'except for the rehearsal. That's why he was late. I don't know how he knew where to look, or what to look for, but he did, and he found him.'

'This,' said Mike, his hand at the blind man's elbow, 'is Heini Spindler.'

'I'm beginning to feel,' said Lucas with a slightly dazed smile, 'that you carry that horn for magic purposes, Mr Brace. Are you sure you didn't just blow it, and summon him?'

Mike looked down at the scuffed leather case, and grinned. 'I didn't have time to take it back to my room after the rehearsal. I had to leave it where I borrowed the bike, and pick it up when I got back. I can't afford to leave it lying about, it's all I've got.'

'You seem to me to need nothing more. It seems I'm infinitely obliged to you, even if I don't quite understand yet what's been going on. And to Herr Spindler, too,' he said, turning to the blind man. 'I remember seeing you once, at least, before, though I didn't know you then. And hearing you, which was also a pleasure. You are the fiddler we were admiring in the procession.'

The blind man tilted his shaggy head and slid off the limp hat into his left hand, holding out the right to Lucas.

'You're the man,' he said, feeling at the fingers he held, his own hand gnarled like the knotty roots of a tree. 'Even your voice I might have known, for all these years. I never forget a voice, it's face and walk and all to me. I had good reason to remember yours. But better than that, here were you with the words in your mouth again that you said to me then. Every word between us I remember. That was the kind of night a man doesn't forget.'

'I'm very grateful,' said Lucas from his heart, and for far more than his life. 'Has Mr Brace told you already what we need from you? Will you be willing to tell the police about that night, and let them write down your statement for you? It would be of the greatest help to me. And to others.'

The lean, beaked face had cocked sideways at the mention of the police, who in the usual way were no particular friends of his. The thought tickled him. He said he would be pleased, and laughed aloud at the irony.

'And you? I hear you got safely away over the mountains that night, and are come home now a great man. You heard my music, shall I hear yours?'

'You shall,' said Lucas, shaken and pleased. 'I'll see to it. And you won't object if the newspapers are allowed to publish what you have to tell?'

'What I say I say for whoever cares to hear.' Being a celebrity was not important to him, but it would be entertaining for once in his life. In his own chosen way he was a celebrity already. Hardly a wedding or a patronal festival in the province was complete without him.

'I'm deeply grateful to you both,' said Lucas, 'and in a quarter of an hour or so I hope to be able to show it. But just now would you mind going away and leaving Crista and me alone for a while? What I think you might do, if you'll be so kind, is to go and call in Hugo Geestler and Richard from their wildgoose-chase in the garden, and tell them we've found our witness, and he's willing to confirm my story just as soon as we can get it into the press. I wonder you managed to bring a boat in and get up here without being challenged—'

'We didn't,' said Una. 'They know we're here, they stopped us right down below, but when they saw who we were they told us to get up into the house quickly, and make sure you stayed in cover. They're still beating the shrubberies.'

It was curiously gratifying to know that they had not let even these allies creep in unchallenged. 'They could stop that now,' he said. 'Please ask them – will you? – not to disturb us just yet, but assure them we're all right.' He met their doubting, respectful eyes calmly, and said: 'Crista was rather upset by the incident, she insisted on locking the door for safety. Don't worry, all she needs is time to recover from the shock.'

And he smiled at Una, so guilelessly that she almost believed him. He was hardly even trying to deceive, only to enlist them all in whatever it was he was doing, and meant to do.

'And please take care of Herr Spindler for me until I come, find him a drink and a meal. Will you go with them? I'll come very soon.'

And to Mike, with the authoritative and tranquil mixture of laughter and gravity that seemed to have come to him as a gift out of this evening's crisis: 'I should think you might blow our friends a fanfare from the terrace, Mr Brace, that should bring them running. Please apologise to them for all the trouble I've caused. And tell them it's at an end.' But how was he ever going to explain away the bullet-hole in Herr Graf's window? Better not even try. Never explain, never – except to two boys erroneously included in the roster of possible assassins – apologise! 'Would you ask them to be so kind as to take a statement from Herr Spindler before I join them? Then I can't be held to have done any prompting.'

'Whatever you say,' said Mike Brace.

They didn't understand, but they obeyed, large-eyed, wondering, but not questioning. Perhaps there was very little they did not dimly perceive, but they knew when to hold their tongues.

'And anything you may have overheard before I opened the door – except for the words Herr Spindler recognised – you will forget,' he said with finality, as they turned towards the door. 'We were going over the facts together, to see if there was some significant point we'd missed. You understand?'

They said, almost truthfully now, that they understood. It was the fiddler who suddenly turned back in the doorway, detaching his arm from Mike's guiding hand to fumble through his pockets.

'I had forgotten – you sent a message by me, and I could not deliver it. They had taken your man away. I knew of no one else who was safe. And then, one did not ask.'

'No,' agreed Lucas, quivering to the too vivid memory, 'one did not ask anything. Not unless one already knew the answer. We shall speak of it soon.'

'Yes, surely. But this – this I give back to you. I could not deliver it, I had no right to destroy it.' He had an instinct for the natural nobility of simple creatures who keep their word once they have given it, who do not hold themselves excused by time or circumstance. 'Now I give it back to you.'

He had found what he was hunting for, in the depths of a cloth wallet stuffed with God-knew-what of personal memories, inarticulate souvenirs, photographs to him invisible. He held it out, after smoothing it attentively between the fingers that did his seeing for him. 'This is the right one. I know it by the edge, and this stamp here – it makes an oval ridge I can feel. This is yours.'

All the rest of them were still, as Lucas took it in his hands, and smoothed it as the fiddler had done, but with a movement that was like a measured and marvelling caress. An oblong card in an old-fashioned cellophane pocket, creased into so fine a network of wrinkles that it half obliterated the limp pasteboard within. There was a flurry of typed details, a printed number, a blue official stamp just infringing the discreet, half-identifiable photograph. All the art of the war years was in that photograph, the ability to be half one person, half another, half on one side and hunting one's own kind, half on the other side, where one's heart and all one's passion converged, with the hunted, helping them over frontiers into safety. The typewritten name, the forged signature, were fictional; but the face, however artfully half-withdrawn, was without question, for those who loved and knew him, Valentine Gelder's face. Lucas could see his daughter there, unbearably poignant and young. And this had been carried for twenty-eight years in the fiddler's wallet, waiting to be delivered or punctiliously returned. A man of his word, once given.

Lucas looked up at them with eyes almost as blind as Blind Heini's, and said quietly:

'Thank you! Leave this with me, now. And go away! Please!'

'But I still don't see,' said Una, slicing onions and tomatoes in the kitchen for a scratch supper all round, 'how you knew he'd be blind.'

She and Mike had the commissariat to themselves, and were sampling the joint experience with a certain amount of curiosity and self-interest, looking to the future. Hugo Geestler and Richard Schwalbe were shut up in the formal dining-room with the fiddler, taking down a lengthy and dramatic statement. Lu would have to deal with their professional suspicions later, but if they were convinced – more important, if Wehrle and Heinz-Otto Graf were convinced – that the trouble was over and would never recur, they might be disposed to meet him halfway. Lu would manage whatever he wanted; Lu with that tone in his voice and that look in his eye could manage anything. Una had a feeling that she ought to be worrying about all that remained unexplained, about the locked door and the tense voices, and Crista's motionless silence in the big chair. But where life was, and truth had declared unmistakably on Lu's side, everything else seemed good and acceptable.

Especially this improbable culinary partnership. Who would have thought Mike would have had such a light hand with a salad dressing?

'I didn't *know*. But I thought he might, from various things your dad had said. His man always said: "I heard", never "I saw". People don't, you know, eyes always take precedence, even in the dark. And then there was the bit about turning his head away while he talked to him, never looking directly at him. People who have to use their ears for eyes often do that. And then it accounted for his not reading the papers at all. An ordinary man would have come forward to tell what he knew. And if he was blind, I hoped he might be someone who didn't go far afield, only around the Tyrol. So then I thought of Blind Heini. Well, I knew him, I'd seen him around, all the fairground gang know him. And he was the right age, and what the hell, it was worth a try. But all morning round the fairground I couldn't find him, and it was only just before rehearsal that I heard he'd gone out to one of the farms to play at a wedding. So I had to go and fetch him out of there – and you can't just rush in and pinch the fiddler, you have to wait until pretty late in the proceedings. And it did take rather a time.'

It hadn't been finding him that had taken the time, but sobering him up sufficiently to get him on a pillion safely, even after his identity and his memory had been put to the test. All that labour with coffee and the farm pump had paid off in the end. Mike didn't grudge it now. Particularly when he contemplated Una in a fresh dress and a nylon apron, flushed and intent, with one eye on the clock and one on her salad.

'He hasn't forgotten anything. Not a thing. He never talked about it much, because even for some years after the war it was still the sort of thing you didn't talk about. But still it was his bomb-story, if you know what I mean. And keeping that legitimation all this time – that's proof positive.'

'I think you've been *marvellous*,' said Una, with a warmth that made his heart somersault in his chest. It was extraordinary how far from brash he felt tonight, handicapped as he was by her natural gratitude. She didn't really feel anything for him, except on her old man's account. It wouldn't do to kid himself.

'You know, Mike,' she said seriously, 'you promised to tell me what it was you didn't want the police to know about you. I mean . . . You know how happy Lu and I would be if there was something *we* could do for *you*.'

'It wasn't the police I minded knowing, it was your old man. Well, there *was* just this thing about running off from Innsbruck without paying my lodgings, but that didn't matter, because I'd sent her the money from here as soon as I drew my first pay, so my nose was clean about that. That was why I was so broke. No, it was your old man who bothered me. Once I told them all that string of addresses, it wouldn't take them long to find out what I was doing, running round on one-week stands and café gigs with a horn. And I didn't want him to know – not until I'd had a chance to show what I could do with straight stuff – that I only really played in a third-rate jazz band. I thought I might be out on my ear again,' he said ruefully, 'if he found out.'

'Mike!' said Una reproachfully, shaken out of her happy housewifely trance by the unaccustomed note of humility in his voice. 'Is *that* all?'

'All? It was enough to fix me. This band of ours,' he said bitterly, 'bust up in Innsbruck. The chap who ran it went off with a girl who sang in the café, and took all our pay with him. I had to sneak off on the sly to come here for an audition, my landlady wouldn't even have let me take my horn if she'd known I was flat broke. Can't blame her, I suppose. But I did send her the money as soon as I landed the job. You can see I needed that job pretty badly, I couldn't afford to get labelled as a small-time jazz player until I was well set. And it wasn't the money, either. That music of your old man's – once I'd got my hands on that I didn't mean to let go. The solo part! And it just dropped in my lap!'

'After all you've done for us,' said Una, pushing back a fistful of fair hair and addressing herself energetically to whisking a bowl of eggs, 'he owes you a special concerto of your own. You can bet nobody's going to be allowed to rob you now – even if you did have to row yourself into the middle of the lake to get in a little secret practice.'

'I didn't do so much,' he said seriously. 'And even if I had, he wouldn't let that influence him, not where music's concerned. If I'm not good enough he'll throw me out on my ear. I wouldn't respect him if he didn't.'

'Don't be silly, of course you're good enough, he thinks you're fine. He said you've got a great future ahead of you, all you've got to do is work at it. You surely don't think you're going back to sleeping rough and working café gigs, after "The Horn of Roland", do you?'

She detected in her own voice, interestingly

enough, the same defensive warmth with which it had
once spoken up, in and out of season, for Lucas. The
one man of all men, as far as she could see from her
last glimpse of him, who was least going to need a
champion from now on.

Mike must have heard something in it to his peculiarly intimate and personal advantage, too, even if he
could not so readily identify it. She turned suddenly to
switch on the top plate of the cooker, and found she
had somehow walked into his arms. It was plain
dreaming clumsiness on his part, not calculation, but
it served the same purpose. His last coherent thought,
before the tide of events carried him away, was that he
hoped her old man wouldn't pop out on them too
soon. He might think this was *con* just a little too
much *brio*!

Lucas relocked the door, and went and sat down on
the arm of Crista's chair, facing her with a tired but
tranquil smile. She neither moved nor spoke; she sat
with eyes fixed in an exhausted stare. Until he touched
her she did not seem to be aware of him; but her senses
within the frozen shell had followed everything, and
he knew it. He laid the identification card in its crazed
plastic cover in her lap.

'This is yours. They'll need to see it, of course. But
it belongs to you.'

By then she did not need it as evidence, he thought;
but she had great need of it as a talisman, something
that could be touched and handled and verified,
something that could justify her and even overflow
into forgiveness for her mother whenever she looked
at it, until the time came when she turned herself
about fully and gave herself to life, and did not need
to look at it ever again. She laid the fingertips of one
hand upon it slowly, not to lift and examine it, more
of a hieratic gesture like touching the king's sceptre
for sanctuary. She saw the name that meant nothing,
and the face that meant everything. The rigor of her

arms and body relaxed a little, the lines of her face lost their icy edges. When he took her gently by the shoulders and drew her towards him she yielded to his hands, and let her forehead rest against his breast. In a little while warmth seemed to come back into her body, and colour into her face, and she softened in his arms, and heaved a great, liberating sigh.

'No one shall touch you,' said Lucas in a quiet, reasonable voice, though he knew that was not what burdened her. 'No one need know anything. Una and the boy won't talk. Tomorrow we'll issue a joint communiqué – the final story, over your name and mine – Valentine. The police will call off the hunt for you – I'll see to that. You think it'll be difficult? You know what they'll be saying? The whole thing has been a well-run publicity stunt for the festival. And everybody'll be satisfied with that.' Still she didn't speak. 'Do you want your gun back?' he asked rather helplessly. 'Or shall I drop it in the lake?'

She shook her head a little, and in a moment words came out of her in painful gasps, like spurts of arterial blood: 'If they'd even let her see him! He knew you – he would have known. She'd have believed him!'

'She's dead now?' he asked gently.

'Two years ago. Women are strange,' she said wonderingly, as though she contemplated a species not her own. 'She never let me rest from hating and blaming you. And yet she married again – only three years after they shot him. Lohr was her name, not mine.'

So much the better, he thought, they won't have traced you yet, and somehow from tomorrow we'll close this, for good. They'll be glad to let it drop, and assume that once the truth was established young Gelder, like a sensible lad, believed it, and dropped his vendetta. And even if they've got as far as discovering that the lad wasn't a lad at all, but a girl, still I think they'll be content to let well alone. He touched her black hair, and it clung quivering to his fingers.

'Crista Valentine Gelder, look at me!'

She lifted her head. He saw a living face again, warm and mobile, though the dark eyes still had their wide, stunned look.

'I should certainly have killed you,' she said, 'if he hadn't come. It's all I was bred for. She always said you'd come back, some day. All I had to do was wait.'

'I know. You needed him even more than I did. But he did come, in time for both of us. I'm alive, and you're absolved. There's nothing to agonise about any more.'

She shook her head, her eyes still searching him through and through, because now she could believe what she saw, and admit what she knew of him, without asking leave of any other creature, living or dead.

'You'd better have that drink now,' he said, relieved to see her stirring into life and feeling again; and he rose, and went to fetch it from where he had set it down for safety when death was only a matter of seconds away from him.

Crista braced her hands upon the arms of the chair and raised herself slowly, watching his straight, slender back walk away from her. She held her father's legitimation in her hands, but it was at Lucas she looked.

In a very low voice she said: 'You won't mind if I stay here until morning? I'll leave early, I promise you won't have to see me again before I go.'

She had had some warning in her heart before she spoke of how terrible the words would sound to her, but she had had no inkling of how profound an effect they would have upon him. He spun round with the glass in his hand, gaping at her in consternation, and his lips shaped: 'Go?' in a soundless gulp. It took him a second or two to recover his voice.

'*Go?*' he repeated, loud and indignant, like a child threatened with abandonment. 'You can't go! I don't want you to go! You're surely not going to desert me now? For God's sake, girl, can't you see you've gone right through into my bones? What should I do without you?'

The words fell between them, dismayed and dismaying. They stood staring at each other like people startled out of sleep, astonished and afraid. They could not speak; they had no idea what was to become of them, and dared not look ahead beyond tomorrow. But he knew and she knew that she would do whatever he asked of her, and that as long as she lived she would never willingly leave him.

More Crime Fiction from Headline:

E L L I S
PETERS

THE PIPER ON
THE MOUNTAIN

DOMINIC FELSE INVESTIGATES

When Herbert Terrell falls off a mountain during his
annual climbing holiday in Czechoslovakia, accidental
death seems the inevitable verdict. But Terrell's young
step-daughter, Tossa, is not the type to bow to the
inevitable. She'd been planning to spend her summer
vacation in Europe in any case, so what could be
simpler than to persuade her companions to make
a minor detour to the scene of the crime?

Not a little bewitched by Tossa's brown eyes, Dominic
Felse is game for a change of plan, though he doesn't at
first suspect her real motive. And he's certainly not
prepared for their innocent touring holiday to become
a deadly game of cat and mouse, with Tossa herself
the unlikely victim . . .

A fragment of an English folk song, the plaintive
lament of a pipe, an unexpected corpse – these are the
clues that the amateur sleuths must solve to discover
the riddle of the piper on the mountain.

Also by Ellis Peters and available from Headline
MOURNING RAGA
DEATH TO THE LANDLORDS

FICTION/CRIME   0 7472 3226 1   £3.99

More compulsive fiction from Headline:

ELLIS PETERS

The author of the bestselling *Brother Cadfael* novels

MOURNING RAGA

AN INDIAN WHODUNNIT

As a favour to his girlfriend Tossa's beautiful but erratic filmstar mother, Dominic Felse agrees to escort a teenage heiress back to her father in India. But travelling with the spoilt, precocious Anjli is no sinecure – and the task of delivering her to her family proves even less easy.

Dominic and Tossa find themselves embroiled in a mystery that swiftly and shockingly becomes a murder investigation. For behind the colourful, smiling mask of India that the tourist sees is another country – remote, mysterious – and often shatteringly brutal . . .

'Strongly plotted story of kidnapping and murder in a well-observed Delhi. Exciting and humane.'
H. R. F. Keating, The Times

FICTION/CRIME   0 7472 3121 4   £2.99

More Crime Fiction from Headline:

E L L I S
PETERS

FUNERAL OF FIGARO
AN OPERATIC WHODUNNIT

When Figaro is killed in an aeroplane crash it seems that nothing can save the production of Mozart's well-loved opera at the Leander Theatre. But then world-class baritone Marc Chatrier arrives from Europe and the cast breathes a sigh of relief. Yet music is not all that is close to the handsome singer's heart, and when he sets his cap at young Hero, the teenage daughter of the Leander's owner, feathers are ruffled.

Somewhat seduced by the unexpected attention, Hero is baffled by the signs of upset among the group, and there seems to be more than petty jealousy afoot. Then Chatrier is killed in the middle of a performance, and it is clear that someone has a particularly vicious dislike of the man, but would anyone resort to murder?

A broken love affair, a wartime betrayal and the respect of a servant for his master are some of the fragments of the past unearthed by Detective Inspector Musgrave in his quest to discover just who is responsible for the funeral of Figaro.

Also by Ellis Peters and available from Headline:
DEATH TO THE LANDLORDS
MOURNING RAGA
THE PIPER ON THE MOUNTAIN
CITY OF GOLD AND SHADOWS

FICTION/CRIME   0 7472 3371 3   £2.99

A selection of bestsellers from Headline

FICTION

THE FIFTH PROFESSION	David Morrell	£4.99 ☐
TABLES	John Lucas	£4.99 ☐
ENTICEMENTS	Una-Mary Parker	£4.99 ☐
OUR FAMILY	Victor Pemberton	£4.50 ☐
FORTUNE	Ritchie Smith	£4.99 ☐
ADVENTURELAND	Steve Harris	£4.99 ☐
PASSION NEVER KNOWS	Adam Kennedy	£4.99 ☐
ARMY BLUE	Lucian K Truscott IV	£4.99 ☐

NON-FICTION

TOM JONES: A Biography	Stafford Hildred & David Gritten	£3.99 ☐
THE FOOD ADDICT'S DIET	Tish Hayton	£3.99 ☐

SCIENCE FICTION AND FANTASY

THE HOUSE OF CTHULHU Tales from The Primal Land Volume Two	Brian Lumley	£3.99 ☐
TALIESIN'S TELLING Daughter of Tintagel 4	Fay Sampson	£3.99 ☐
THE CRYSTAL KEEP	Sheila Gilluly	£4.99 ☐

All Headline books are available at your local bookshop or newsagent, or can be ordered direct from the publisher. Just tick the titles you want and fill in the form below. Prices and availability subject to change without notice.

Headline Book Publishing PLC, Cash Sales Department, PO Box 11, Falmouth, Cornwall, TR10 9EN, England.

Please enclose a cheque or postal order to the value of the cover price and allow the following for postage and packing:
UK: 80p for the first book and 20p for each additional book ordered up to a maximum charge of £2.00
BFPO: 80p for the first book and 20p for each additional book
OVERSEAS & EIRE: £1.50 for the first book, £1.00 for the second book and 30p for each subsequent book.

Name ....

Address ....

....

....